I0614334

HIDDEN
IN IRISH
HILLS

HIDDEN
IN IRISH
HILLS

MARY CATES

AMBASSADOR INTERNATIONAL
GREENVILLE, SOUTH CAROLINA & BELFAST, NORTHERN IRELAND

www.ambassador-international.com

Hidden in Irish Hills: A Novel

©2021 by Mary Cates
All rights reserved

ISBN: 978-1-64960-108-7
eISBN: 978-1-64960-158-2
Library of Congress Control Number: 2021940392

Editing by Michelle Wyatt
Cover design by Hannah Linder Designs
Interior typesetting by Dentelle Design
Digital Edition by Anna Riebe Raats

Scripture taken from *The Living Bible* copyright © 1971 by Tyndale House Foundation. Used by permission of Tyndale House Publishers Inc., Carol Stream, Illinois 60188. All rights reserved.

No part of this publication may be reproduced, distributed, or transmitted in any form or by any means, including photocopying, recording, or other electronic or mechanical methods, without the prior written permission of the publisher, except in the case of brief quotations embodied in critical reviews and certain other noncommercial uses permitted by copyright law. For permission requests, contact the publisher using the information below.

This is a work of fiction. Names, characters, and incidents are all products of the author's imagination or are used for fictional purposes. Any resemblance to actual events or persons, living or dead, is entirely coincidental. Any mentioned brand names, places, and trademarks remain the property of their respective owners, bear no association with the author or the publisher, and are used for fictional purposes only.

AMBASSADOR INTERNATIONAL
Emerald House
411 University Ridge, Suite B14
Greenville, SC 29601, USA
www.ambassador-international.com

AMBASSADOR BOOKS
The Mount
2 Woodstock Link
Belfast, BT6 8DD, Northern Ireland, UK
www.ambassadormedia.co.uk

The colophon is a trademark of Ambassador, a Christian publishing company.

CHAPTER 1

THE PLAN

EVERYTHING WAS CALM AT THE Carson mansion in the Irish Hills, at least for the moment. The mansion was Rachael's quiet hideaway in Michigan, far from the New York penthouse and her corporate real estate office. But yesterday, breaking news on the television screen interrupted her tranquil leisure, sending her into a wild frenzy of chilled nerves. One moment she was enjoying peaceful relaxation, the next her hands turned ice cold, and her heart beat rapidly. The news anchor announced a sudden war was breaking out in the Mediterranean. While she listened to the news, she remembered that her husband, Grant Garrison, forewarned of this war long ago.

It was mid-morning, and hearing the announcement set her in a mode of alertness and cast a shadow over the entire day, most likely for the rest of her life. The challenges in her future would now prove to be the greatest she and Grant, and the entire world for that matter, would ever again face. She grabbed hold of the phone and called him.

******

Grant was seventy miles away at Holton Computer Corporation on the tenth floor of the Renaissance Center in downtown Detroit. He was unaware of the news Rachael was bearing. Ironically, he was

5

planning this very day to have a serious word with his boss, Archer Holton, regarding the computer software program the corporation was creating. Grant discovered it was a monster of a program, with evil potential that had to be stopped before it could take over the world like an octopus crawling over a swarm of crayfish on the bottom of the ocean. He became aware of its impending immoral capacity shortly after he started working there, but stopping it would be no easy feat. He understood that no one challenged the corporation without suffering Archer's uncontrolled vengeance, including ill fate.

While the morning continued, Grant found himself getting anxious while he waited for the right moment to confront Archer. Each hour that passed he watched and waited for an opportunity to walk into Archer's office and have it out with him. Regardless of the consequences, he was compelled to speak against this madness of creating a computer system that could govern world finances and keep track of every person on earth. Archer Holton's software program was a universal nightmare for every person that loved liberty and freedom. Rebuking him would churn up a fury worse than hell. Still, he had to do something, even if by some mysterious plan, the software might be fitting perfectly into God's design for planet Earth.

Acting like a scared dog with its tail tucked between his hind legs was never Greg's style. On the contrary, he was a man of inner strength, and he never cowered when it came to a choice between right or wrong. He could not compromise his moral convictions after discovering the evil mixed into this software, not even for the sake of a lucrative paycheck. His wealth in the Carson Real Estate Corporation with Rachael did not influence or oblige this additional income from the Holton Computer Technology Corporation. He was simply a computer ace, doing what he thought was a favor for the Holton Corporation.

It was all so innocent the way it started, like an angel of light handing him a phenomenal opportunity to use his genius in the computer arena. Who would have thought the devil was behind what they sought from him. Without any suspicion, Grant was immediately impressed with the Holton outfit. He was happy to use his computer genius in an independent computer software company that was on the cutting edge of technology. Holton's office was located at Detroit's downtown waterfront. Everything seemed great, but after working with this company for a few months, he discovered a cynical madness that reeked of evil power.

Archer had a concept bouncing around in his head that was steps ahead of global politics. He called his idea mesh-working. When put into operation, it would spin the world on a new axis. The software would open the door for a connecting computer service worldwide through which a common financial system could be used. It fit perfectly into the plans of The Great Ten Nations, a powerful conglomerate of nations pressing for world dominance.

Archer chaperoned every detail of his brainchild with absolute authority and ruled his company with an iron fist. His elephantine ego went hand and hand with his tyrant behavior. Set-backs were not accepted, and anyone who dared challenge him was terminated on the spot. He was an egomaniac who rarely acted civilized toward anyone. Although his employees were professional wizards at their craft, they were mere subordinates. He insulted them on a daily basis. He kept everyone in line and insisted they work at a fever pitch. His work demands made him look important, like someone who could drop the atom bomb if he chose. He was a browbeater with ugly behavior that popped up in childish fits of anger when things were not moving fast. He reminded Grant of the neighborhood bully who sent kids home crying to their mothers rather than play by the rules. His staff tolerated him only because he paid big-buck salaries.

Grant's courage on this breaking news day was stalwart, though he was unaware at this moment of the war outbreak in the Mediterranean. He simply stuck to his work, watching the clock and observing office activity, waiting for a nudge in his gut that signaled the right moment to walk into Archer's office. In his mind, his speech was planned. There would be no negotiating, for there was no such thing as parleying with the devil. The talk would be tough, and his verbal attack would confront Archer head-on and lead into the criminal effect the software would have on the world population. There was nothing to lose except his life, which seemed unimportant when stacked up against wicked foul play. Grant was aware that Archer could do away with him with the snap of his fingers and a nod to one of his cronies. But he would take the risk because he could not sit back and let this madman deliver a project into the hands of these evil world dictators.

It was less than a year ago, at a software seminar that Archer ran into Grant and enticed him to work a short-term contract. He offered him the position of Director of Implementations. Grant had no clue that he was being asked to work on a software monopoly. So at first, he was thrilled with the new position. The work challenged his keen computer skills and brought tons of self-gratification. But less than six months into the new position he began to see the devious side of the software program. He realized that his employer's creation was a beastly system that would deplete identification of the working class.

During weekly staff meetings, the chief goal was to produce credible ideas for faster and broader computer technology. Making it worse was Archer's frantic drive to get this project completed immediately because it was driven by a government mandate, given secretively to him months ago.

It was incredible how fast the work progressed and how unbelievable this group of computer wizards could tuck themselves away and not recognize the evil force driving every move. This guru was designing a suffocating creation whose end purpose would thwart capitalism. It would bring America to its knees; essentially it would bring the whole world to its knees. But Archer's staff was so lost in their progressive ignorance that evil was having a field day right there in the center of downtown Detroit.

If he pulled this thing off and the dictators of the world fully embraced his software, then the world population would be cataloged. The government would know everyone's personal business investments, religious beliefs, club affiliations, and ethnic background. The software would generate the power to regulate every business transaction that involved buying and selling. It was a plan that reeked of Stalinism, but a sure bet for Archer, who seemed oblivious to its consequences. In his mind he would soon become a self-proclaimed goodwill ambassador, selling his invention as a protective plan against fraud and collusion, when in reality it was an evil system from hell.

Of course, there would be skeptics who would question the new program, but this ideology would come to pass and be used worldwide for the simple reason that the population was sick and tired of terrorist's attacks, ethnic cleansings, cop killings, torture, disrespectful protests, and rage of every kind. The world seemed to be awaiting a Caesar and a promised land of safety and security. Archer had the blueprint and was creating something keenly acceptable for the fearful multitudes. The new global coalition—those ten nations hungry for power—would soon come on the scene.

******

As Rachael's day was beginning in the Irish Hills, before the news alert, the day was coming up spectacular. Brilliant sunlight was cascading over the rolling knolls like aerobic waves rising and falling in rhythmic tempo. Rachael awoke and slid her hand along the silk sheet to touch Grant, but he wasn't there. Panic shot through her body like a bolt of lightning. She was sure he would quietly slip into bed last night without waking her. Something was wrong! Throwing the covers back, she leaped out of bed and grabbed her robe, halfway pushing her feet into slippers. Duke opened his eyes but stayed curled at the foot of the bed. Wasting no time, she dashed down the massive staircase and bolted into the kitchen, finding her maids, Maggie and Lillian, sipping coffee and discussing their duties for the day.

"Land sakes child, you look like someone who missed the last train out," Maggie said, while Rachael held onto the back of Lillian's chair, catching her breath.

"Grant didn't come home last night, and he didn't call. Something has happened to him," she blurted out.

Seeing the wild terror in her eyes and hearing her hysterical tone, Maggie tried to remain calm while Rachael continued to talk.

"Forget about what you're doing today, you've got to go with me to Detroit," she said, looking straight at Maggie as if her command was a decree ordered by God.

Maggie got up from her chair and walked to the counter, deliberately trying to gain control of what might be an over-reaction from Rachael. She took an orange from the fruit bowl and turned toward her.

"Rachael, honey, have you tried calling him this morning?"

"I tried calling all last evening," she responded. "I fell asleep, knowing he would either call or come in late. Something has happened—something terrible, I just feel it."

Lillian got up from the table and poured a cup of coffee.

"Maybe he went to your Dearborn condo last night—maybe it was too late to call," she suggested.

Dead sure that Grant would never neglect calling her unless something was terribly wrong, Rachael nervously pushed Grant's numbers on the kitchen phone. Still, there was no answer at the condo. She dialed his cell number, but it offered only a response to leave a message.

"Something has happened to him," she said in desperation. "I feel it so strongly."

Without waiting for them to comment further, she related the evening news to them about the sudden military action in the Mediterranean—coupling her spiel with spattered bits about Holton Computer Corporation and its owner, Archer Holton. Maggie and Lillian knew nothing about this new war because they had the day off and returned to their second-floor quarters in the mansion long after Rachael had gone to bed.

The news of the sudden war jolted Maggie, although she was well aware of tense world conditions and the possibility that anything could happen at any given moment. Rachael and Grant's philosophy, of which Maggie knew about, centered upon a global apex occurring suddenly by military force. It had been discussed with her in detail many times because they knew it would happen one day soon. They convinced her that warfare would eventually change the course of the world. But to hear that The Great Ten Nations were now in the process of moving forward with their contrived takeover sent a chill through her like death itself. She waited for Rachael to continue talking, but the young woman stood mute, as though the moment were too terrifying to speak further.

"This may be the beginning of what you and Grant have warned about, Miss Rachael," Maggie soberly said, noticing Lillian watching both their reactions with curious interest.

Lillian was not easily alarmed about anything, but her lack of enthusiasm wasn't because she was stupid. She was a bona fide skeptic. If a salesman knocked at the kitchen door and demonstrated a vacuum cleaner with a powerful motor that purred like a kitten, she would challenge his pitch and say it probably couldn't pick up a dead fly off a slick hardwood floor. Her opinion of Rachael and Maggie's belief that The Great Ten Nations of the world were getting ready to take over the globe through a wild shadowy financial system was nothing more than an opinion. She heard the word Armageddon tossed around in the news media and watched the famous movie about the end of the world, but she didn't believe a great war would occur, or that a skirmish in the Mediterranean would change the course of mankind.

"Everything fits," Maggie continued, while Lillian slowly trickled cream into the cup of coffee and offered it to Rachael, but the young woman's trembling lips were far from fancying coffee.

"Maggie, get your purse and drive my car around to the front door," Rachael commanded while walking out of the kitchen. "I'll be down in a minute, as soon as I get dressed. Lillian, you stay here in case Grant calls or comes home while we are gone."

Maggie knew her place was at Rachael's side, a place she earned through years of loyal service to the Carson family. Twelve years ago, she clandestinely emerged as the foster matriarch when Rachael's mother died suddenly. Yet her revered position was not simply attributed to the untimely death of Catherine Carson, but to her personal appointment with destiny. As far as Maggie was concerned, Divine providence inescapably provided the path for her to love and serve this wealthy family, long before they encountered each other.

AFTER CATHERINE'S SUDDEN DEATH, IT seemed only fitting that Maggie focus her love on Rachael. From the moment Catherine winged her way out of this world in a head-on car collision, Maggie took Rachael under her care, as though she were her very own. The young college graduate responded to her instinctively, generating a loving and unique relationship between them.

Some say white, rich people are prejudiced, but it didn't matter to Rachael that Maggie was black—that she came from an indigent family and that she was a hired servant. Maggie was anything but common. The woman's heart was full of love, and her possession of Godly wisdom encircled everything she said and did.

Although she was careful to stay within the bounds of her position, those margins never interfered with her unfailing compassion. She became the understanding ear her young mistress often required. She was the hug, the praise, the encouragement that the young girl needed. Maggie was everything Rachael missed from her mother. It seemed certain that Divine providence played the biggest role in Maggie's destiny from the moment she decided to come to New York City, a destiny to serve a wealthy family and enjoy a life of refinement within their plush quarters. It was no coincidence that she wanted more than the same life of her parents. It was no twist of fate that she found Rachael in New York City.

******

The story of Maggie is that she was once a poor girl, solely destined to inherit the same banal existence of her parents in the ghetto of Saginaw. But an unexplained persuasion existed in her mind that something beyond the cookie-cutter life she was doomed to follow was calling her to something more.

It was late spring, 1943, when sixteen-year-old Maggie ventured into an electrified tent revival meeting in the heart of Saginaw. And though she was what some might dub an unspiritual vagabond, considering that her behavior was seriously delinquent of religion, she had a gnawing desire to have a clear conscience with God. There was no question that she knew right from wrong and that God was not pleased with her for sneaking out of the house to be with boys, stealing her father's cigarettes, and skipping school whenever she felt like it. Although behaviors like these were common among teenagers in the ghetto, it was her conscience that never justified her behavior.

Exactly what it was that spawned her remorse, she wasn't sure, but she knew there had to be a Person up there in Heaven watching everything she did. Her grandma-maw would say it was the Holy Ghost doing its office work in her heart that was convicting her. Whatever it was, be it pure condemnation or fear of getting caught, it didn't matter, because the teenager needed to find peace with God. But rather than listen to her spiritual grandma-maw, she instead drifted further away. So, quite unexpectedly, this outdoor church service would become her answer. At least it was a momentary thought that drove her into the tent to check things out.

Walking through the open flaps, the smell of the musty canvas was sickening. She made an ugly face and pinched her nose closed but kept moving inside. The meeting was underway, and every chair in the back rows was taken. The congregation looked to her like a white person's convention where she probably wasn't welcome. But tonight she was adventurous, maybe even a bit brazen, so she walked several rows toward the front and deliberately inched into a seat next to an old white woman, daring anyone to usher her out.

The music was loud and created an electrifying atmosphere that stirred up lots of excitement. Maggie's heart was beating as fast as the music, and her stomach was churning. She felt frightened. Perhaps she had made a huge mistake by entering this stinking tent. The place was anything but reverent, and she was sure it was far too unrefined for God to have anything to do with it. But she couldn't bring herself to get up and walk out. Instead, the thought that God must be there kept her seated.

By all accounts she should be questioning her sanity, but the old white lady softened the scene by smiling at her. Now she was trapped to the bitter end, whatever that would be.

The truth of the matter was that if it were not for her spiritual craving and all the curious chatter about this tent revival at the Garden Café, where she washed dishes after school, she would not be there. Something more than fate had beckoned her.

The old lady moved her purse closer to her feet and smiled again. Maggie straightened her wrinkled greased-spotted dress and breathed in the stale air. The scene would be humorous, if one could find humor in a poor black teenager cocksure that she had a right to sit next to a proper old white woman and hope God would be aware of her sincerity.

Her dark skin stood out like a grubby goat among a flock of sheep. She wished her skin wasn't black and that her life wasn't loaded down with wishes, wishes for things she would never have unless she stole them or did something immoral to get them. Simply put, she was born bankrupt by the misfortune of having roots in a poor Negro family, and if God didn't do something to help her, she was lost. Her heritage had its roots in Louisiana, where her great-grandparents lived as poor children of slaves. She was an offspring of human failure, a girl whose ignoble genealogy offered little hope to become more than a white employer's domestic subordinate. But she didn't want anyone's pity because her stubborn arrogance instilled a tenacious unwillingness to yield to the pathetic patterns of her relatives. If one dared to say that good comes out of arrogance, then the debate would end because she knew she was as important as any pompous blue-blooded king, or any Hollywood starlet—or for that matter, as important as this little white lady sitting next to her. There was no way this young girl would end up like her mother, swabbing toilets and mopping floors in a public place.

Something mysterious, but very genuine happened in her soul that night. It wasn't a superficial *Jesus moment* like some have when promising God if He'll get them out of a jam they'll change their way of living. No, it was a genuine transformation. By the time the fire and brimstone sermon was delivered, she had genuinely confessed her sins and asked to be forgiven. In that hour—those few moments—her life was changed. Exactly what happened, she was not quite sure because she had no religious background to explain it. She reckoned that she had become a true Believer in Jesus.

The weeks and months passed circumspectly. Maggie continued washing dishes after school and saving paychecks. She safely hid her dollars, retrieving them often to count and dream of leaving the ghetto after graduation. It was no puny dream she had floating around in her brain. She would soon be taking a three-hour bus ride to Detroit, and from there she would transfer to another bus that would take her to New York's Manhattan Island.

New York was the biggest, noisiest city she had ever witnessed. Tall buildings, taxies, and the smell of diesel fuel, all of it reeking with opportunity. Only eighteen years old, she stepped onto the busy sidewalks, clutching her tattered suitcase.

She found work at the Waldorf Astoria Hotel, in the laundry room. Sweaty hard work that paid for her rent in a shabby apartment building and gave her enough money to eat. It was nothing like she imagined. But one day, as God would continue directing with His plan for her life, she answered an ad for a domestic maid to work in a luxurious apartment building on Park Avenue. It was at the Carson's penthouse apartment where she went to interview for the job.

There was an immediate meeting of the minds between Rachael's mother, Catherine, during the interview, and Maggie landed the job. The charisma that sparked between them was mystifying, as though it was ordained. Her destiny launched into motion that day and gave her a pathway out of the futile future in the ghetto.

******

Unsure of whether to go to the Dearborn condo first or to the Holton Computer office at the Renaissance Center, Rachael kept driving east toward the Motor City, leaving the quiet Irish Hills behind. Maggie attempted to make small talk, but nothing she said could smother their fear.

"Try Archer's office number again, Maggie," Rachael said, handing her the cell phone. She rattled off the numbers. Maggie waited until the connection was made and then handed the phone back. A recording started, "the office is closed until nine o'clock."

"Nuts!" Rachael said, slamming the phone down on the car seat.

"I think we should check the Dearborn condo first. If Grant isn't there, then we'll go downtown to the office. By that time, someone should be there."

The sun was full of dazzling brilliance by the time they reached the city limits of Dearborn. Maggie commented about how gorgeous the azure sky was and how the puffy clouds resembled giant cotton balls. It was small talk to help mask her fear that Grant might not be at the condo. She understood Rachael's fear, that he was working in the midst of an evil corporation and her gut reaction was that something terrible had happened to him. Many times she overheard conversations between them about the computer software Holton was creating. She knew that Grant would eventually speak out about it.

The I-75 Interstate was crammed with rushing travelers. Everything seemed normal, as though only Rachael and Maggie knew what the world was facing.

"I can't believe this," Rachael said, pounding the steering wheel with the palm of her hands in disgust. "At this very moment we have the bordering nations of the Mediterranean Sea in the throes of a pending dictatorship and the world is about to become changed forever, but look, no one appears the least bit concerned. Everyone is speeding on their happy way, heading to their jobs, listening to music. Mothers are taking their children to school like the world is at ease and will go on forever."

Maggie shook her head in agreement.

"It's just like you said before," she commented, "the world will be eating and drinking when freedom is ended."

Rachael nodded her head and let her thoughts move back to yesterday's happenings . . .

******

She remembered her hysterical discussion with Grant after hearing the news report of the sudden military action in the Mediterranean . . .

"GARRISON HERE, HOW CAN I help you?" Grant said, answering his extension.

"Grant, you'll never believe what is happening!" Rachael blurted out.

"What's that?"

"There's a sudden war going on. Sources are confirming to the Global News Network that aircraft carriers and special troops are operating in the southern areas of the Mediterranean Sea under the orders of The Great Ten Nations. It's just like we imagined."

Grant interrupted abruptly, "Who's involved?"

"Well, it happened suddenly, like in the blink of an eye. Algeria, Libya, Egypt, and Jordan. They're all under a military-forced overthrow, and it looks to me like the war will move west into Europe. The enemy set everything up methodically. It's just like we figured.

I'm sure the coalition is getting ready to induct their political crusade for world economic conformity. No nuclear bombs were used, but I'm sure they will be threatening if they're needed. It was a sudden takeover. It won't be long before every nation is on its knees. The threat of nuclear warfare is real. Once this starts, they won't stop."

She was crying now, and as she continued her conversation, Grant was stunned. This was the beginning of a world-wide government overthrow that he and Rachael knew was coming. Nevertheless, the news was shocking. Her conversation with him went on.

"The sea has been polluted by Arabian ships that were in the process of transporting oil. They were hit by scud missiles. Reports coming out of the area say that smoke from blazing petroleum is filling the entire region. Oh Grant, it is terrible! Debris and even bodies from the Arabian ships are afloat in the toxic waters. Missiles and shells are striking everywhere, and it's unfolding on the television right before my eyes. You will not believe this, our President is standing down and letting this happen!"

"God help us!" Grant whispered.

Her thoughts kept going . . .

"RIGHT NOW," SHE CONTINUED, "THE news is coming from a correspondent stationed in Egypt, near the Suez Canal. He's telling the world that it happened suddenly. It was a swift attack. The southern areas of the Mediterranean Sea are totally spoiled from strategically aimed bombs. In one fail swoop, they are managing to scare the world into subordination. I mean, that's exactly what's happening, don't you think?"

******

She recalled Grant saying he needed to see Archer right away, that he wanted to try and get the software program stopped.

Her awareness of Grant's suspicions of the Holton Computer Corporation were right on the mark. Getting nations and kingdoms on their knees first and then accomplishing their global plan of world peace under a common system was the ultimate goal of The Great Ten Nations. Confronting Archer was risky, but she knew Grant had to do something, even if it meant to bash the computers into pieces, if that were possible.

******

The Holton Computer Corporation was magnificently stationed in a plush office high in the Renaissance Center. It had mammoth windows that allowed a wide-angled view of the Detroit River Channel below. From this premier waterfront landmark, the striking skyline of Windsor, Ontario could be seen. The thriving downtown area was the hub of on-going business in Detroit. The Renaissance Center seemed the most innocent and perfect locale in which Archer's employees could work. Surrounded by other businesses, and with numerous people working demanding hours and schedules would keep them protected, simply because no one cared what anyone else was doing.

But Archer would never entertain any thought that would stop his software creation. So the expected response was no surprise to Grant when he walked into Archer's office.

"Get out!" Archer shouted. "Don't let the door hit you on the way out!" he yelled at the top of his voice.

Turning as he walked to the door, Grant yelled back, "It's a fatal appointment with kismet! Your scheme will suck the joy out of every goal-seeking person!"

Archer reached for his phone as the door slammed shut.

The confrontation was over. Grant walked back to his desk and slunk into his chair, sweating, fuming, defeated. His explosion put him in great jeopardy. Getting out and into his car would not be easy. He was now being watched by everyone. The best thing to do was to keep himself busy and play-act that the whole ball of wax with him and Archer was oblivious to everyone.

Every move he made, however, was observed. Even a trip to the restroom was accompanied by one of Archer's cronies, who were always there, like Secret Service. Maybe when everyone walked to the conference room for the weekly brainstorming meeting, he could slip out. But no, he would be too visible walking to the elevators. *All I need*, he thought to himself, *is just thirty seconds. Come on, God, give me just thirty seconds, and I can make it out of here!*

Meanwhile, the news of the military action in the Middle East had reached the ears of Archer and his employees. Grant paid no attention but kept his face to the computer screen in front of him, still keeping an eye out for an opportunity to escape. At one o'clock he took his usual seat in the conference room for the brainstorming session. No one appeared to notice how nervous he was opening his briefcase or how clumsily he was spreading his papers out in front of him. He poured a glass of ice water, took a sip, and glanced out the massive wall of windows in front of him. Across the river channel, Ontario looked like heaven off in the distance. If only he could reach it. His plastic facial façade and carefully measured moves helped distract from his fear of being killed for rebuking Archer. But he was truly scared and shaken, knowing that Archer had already tipped off his hit man. Unless he could escape fast and lose his stalker, he would surely be shot somewhere on a squalid city street.

He looked at his cell phone resting amid the papers stacked in front of him, wishing he could pick it up and call Rachael. But no, even if he had the opportunity, he would never call and upset her more. He would talk to her as soon as he was free.

If ideas were hot and changes in technology were decided upon, brainstorming meetings went far into the evening hours. Tonight was no exception, and worse yet, it was getting dark. Perfect *carte du jour* to be assassinated on the shadowy streets of Detroit.

At six o'clock Archer directed his secretary, Annie, to order pizza from Mamma Previno's Italian Restaurant on the ground floor of the Renaissance Center. She could then go home and everyone would take a breather to relax and stretch. Then work would start again. The sighs of relief were like recharging low batteries. Everyone got up out of their chairs.

The elevators and the stairway were accessible from the main hallway, just a few feet from the conference room. Grant watched as the momentary break triggered a tired flow of worn-out executives filing across the hall to the restroom. He noted who had gone out and who had come back, watching for a chance to slip into the hall without being noticed, but no opportunity came. He waited for Archer to get up, hoping that while he was using the restroom, he could escape to the elevators. But Archer stayed seated, puffing on a cigar and laughing at his own senseless jokes with the company's financial officer, who was an obnoxious smooch. At Archer's fingertips was a phone obviously ready to be used if Grant dared to leave. There was no escape. Even a trip to the coffee machine at the back of the room gained the madman's attention.

Annie came in with a large tray loaded with cold sweating cans of Pepsi. Her balance slipped as she leaned into the table with the tray, knocking over a water pitcher and sending a stream of icy water running down the table right into Archer's lap. The madman leaped to his feet, spewing a few choice words while brushing the water droplets off his pants. Others grabbed napkins and helped sop up the mess. This was the chance Grant needed. He quickly sprang from his chair and dashed down the hall to the stairway.

Barreling through the stairway door, he began a frantic run down nine flights of stairs to the parking structure, opting not to wait for the elevator. He could not gamble for a faster exit by losing even a second waiting for the elevator. With lightning speed, he propelled himself down the staircase, feeling as though he were in a fast-moving dream that had quickly turned into a hideous nightmare. He passed the eighth floor and then the seventh. On and on with great speed until he reached the ground floor and the parking structure. He catapulted out the door and made a frantic dash to his car. In seconds, he was squealing around the sharp turns that led outside and onto the dark streets of downtown Detroit.

He raced for the expressway interchange that would lead out of the heart of the city and to Dearborn. He realized that he had managed to get out of Archer's meeting, down nine floors, and into his car in split-second timing. He mopped the sweat from his brow and drove steadily southwest, checking his rearview mirror often, knowing that a hit man was probably on his way. His cell phone was left in the conference room so there was no chance to call Rachael and let her know what was happening. All he had in his possession was the car keys and the wallet tucked in his back pocket.

The perfect place for him to escape to was the mansion in the Irish Hills. It was far away and unknown to Archer, but if he were being followed, it would be dangerous to lead Archer's hit man there. The Dearborn condo was his best bet for safety.

He drove fast enough to be stopped by police, hoping to see a flashing light and hear a screeching siren, but there wasn't a scout car to be seen. He kept racing onward, darting in and out of traffic, hoping to reach the condo before a bullet hit the back window and pelted into his brain.

He reached Dearborn and made a quick turn onto Miller Street, then another screeching two-wheeled turn that took him within sight of the condo. Holding the steering wheel with one hand, he pushed the garage door opener on the visor and raced up the driveway. As soon as he could get inside the condo, he would call Rachael on the land phone and let her know what happened.

******

Rachael swallowed hard and kept driving into the sunlight and the city limits of Dearborn, struggling to shake off the fear. She remembered how lonely the mansion was last night before she went to bed. Maggie and Lillian had spent the day sightseeing and shopping in nearby Toledo and were late returning home. Their absence, along with the news about the Mediterranean conflict, made the cold chill of fear seem worse. Alone, with no one to talk to, she had nothing else to do but think of the dire situation that both Archer Holton and The Great Ten Nations had suddenly brought upon the world.

She understood the evil plan. It was a plan contrived by ten nations: the US, Canada, Great Britain, China, Germany, France, Spain, Italy, Iran, and Russia. Wealth would be distributed equally among the masses of the world, and the pockets of the evildoers would be bulging. Each government would take control of all financial transactions by instituting the world-wide system Archer was working on, and thus control all services and sales. Class superiority would be dissolved. At the same time, the government would create a single avenue for all legal tender by using the Internet. Hence, Archer's brainchild in action. The world would literally become a village under siege.

The whole operation reminded Rachael of a massive mafia takeover, with America playing godfather.

Everything would take place in precise succession. She reckoned that Grant had been intentionally introduced to Archer by a higher power. But for what purpose? Perhaps the truth might be that Grant was actually helping God stop this torrent of madness. Could she dare have such a grandiose thought? A rational theologian might have something different to say. More likely she and Grant were witnessing the fulfillment of End Time prophecy, and her husband's dealings with Holton were predestined for the sole intention of igniting God's purpose at the mansion in the Irish Hills.

Sane thinking gave both Rachael and Grant perfect perception, whether it was theologically proven or not. The truth was that this world system Archer was creating would gobble up everything they owned once it came into play, unless they liquidated their assets and set up escrow accounts for utilities and taxes. Doing this was the only way they could safeguard their wealth and continue in the independence each of them had grown to love. Although the consequences of not complying with the world plan would be severe, Rachael was more than determined to hold on to what she inherited from her deceased parents.

Carson Real Estate was a multi-million-dollar firm her father had built through hard work and brilliancy. No way would she let go of the wealth he had created. If it took every ounce of energy and every breath of life from her, she would work to keep it. If she lost it, she would also lose her ability to help save others. It was understood that, when evil began its final takeover, she and Grant would follow their plan of survival and help others.

Their mansion on Carson Hill made the perfect place for the secret mission they planned. The hill overlooked acres of fertile farmland and small lakes. The mansion was built for Rachael's parents, Walter and Catherine, to serve as their private resort as well as a retreat from the company's headquarters in New York City. Although they loved their Park Avenue penthouse, the mansion in the Irish Hills was like paradise.

The estate consisted of a huge mansion with several off-set adjoining garages, horse stables, and gardens. Densely wooded acreage virtually hid the mansion from easy sight. The property became known to the community as Carson Hill. Below the hill, Springfield Lake stretched six miles in length and three miles broad. Quaint cottages and attractive year-round homes fashionably speckled the shoreline. Catherine loved the Irish Hills hideaway. From its completion in the early 1950s until her death, she spent many years of pleasure there, commuting back and forth, sometimes on a moment's notice. Often she caught a plane out of the LaGuardia Airport and then flew back to New York days later from Detroit's International Airport.

She dabbled in the lavish flower gardens, walked in the woods, and strolled the long brick walkway that led to the stables. On occasion she rode their quarter horses. Nothing felt or smelled better than the crystal air at Carson Hill. In the summer months, Catherine and Rachael loved sitting on the spacious front porch, observing the birds and squirrels from behind the great pillars. What amused them most was the small wildlife that dared to frolic and flirt with them. The clean, crisp country air, so much purer than the stuffy dirty air of New York City, made the days they spent on Carson Hill seem like another world, maybe even heaven. The only intrusive sounds came from occasional cars traveling on the road below, or a farmer's tractor off in the far distance. In the fall, squawking Canadian geese flew overhead, waking them early in the morning. Yet, those sounds were like music compared to the honking horns of taxies in the city that never slept. Catherine and Rachael loved everything about Carson Hill, its sights and sounds, and the wonderful aroma.

Catherine often stayed at the mansion for long periods of time during Rachael's school years, when holidays and summer vacations allowed it. Maggie accompanied them while Lillian stayed at the penthouse and kept things in order for Walter. In a hundred years, no one would have dreamed that this serene landscape in the Irish Hills would be the place where Rachael's mother would meet a sudden violent death. But ironically, it was just that. Twelve years ago, and only ten miles from the mansion, Catherine died in a head-on collision on a two-lane country highway. It was the same year Rachael graduated from New York University.

WALTER NEVER REMARRIED. INSTEAD, HE worked feverishly to build their empire into a revered multi-million dollar business, branding the Carson Real Estate Corporation as one of the most astute and commanding firms in the country. He taught Rachael all he knew about real estate, and she learned quickly by accompanying him whenever he was closing big deals. As time went on, she managed some of their most lucrative contracts. To her daddy's delight, she raked in multi-million dollar sales as though she were the kingpin of their company. Rachael grew into a beautiful young woman, but like some fairy tales end, Walter died of complications after a massive stroke, leaving her alone, except for Maggie.

Strange it was that her parent's deaths were marked by gross dissimilarity. Her mother's death was sudden and premature. She died, leaving Rachael with a gaping hole in her heart. Death became Rachael's enemy, the bearer of sorrow and loneliness. But her father's passing, years later, was different. He was elderly and in bad health. His death was natural. There was not a hint of morbidity in his room the night he passed away. Instead, she witnessed a wonderful transient event, the ending chapter of a man's life, leaving this world in peace and without a struggle. Silently he winged his way heavenward to the God who loved him and had guided him all his life.

Rachael had often thought of him since his death, and last night while she was alone in the mansion, struggling with the news of war, he came to her mind again. Her trembling heart longed to hear his comforting voice echo in the mansion. She wanted to be his little girl again, sitting on his lap. She wanted his strong arms around her, his kiss on her cheek. Comfort was present only in her memory of him.

The lonely moments in the mansion last evening sparked many memories while she waited for Grant to call. She thought about her father's wine cellar in the basement of the mansion. Vividly, she remembered her mother's fundamental Christian faith and how she severely frowned upon alcohol. She would not partake of her husband's vintage wine collection but often joked that the basement cubby was the family's bomb shelter. And it could have been just that, for during the cold war years, and just prior to the building of the mansion, Americans constructed home bomb shelters, and children endured practice air raids at school.

The wine cubby was a special place that had attracted Rachael's youthful attention long before she began to have premonitions about global warfare and the destruction of America's liberty. The cellar was built with thick cement walls, like a mighty bulwark. It had its own thermostat to keep wine at the perfect temperature. The cool dark cellar was a most interesting place for a curious child. Shelf upon shelf was filled with wines of distinction and value, all of them packed into the ten by thirty-foot cement vault. Walter was almost as proud of his costly wine collection as he was his real estate corporation. Rachael felt safe whenever she was in the cellar. It was a solidly built cubby, and she knew it would give them protection if ever they needed it. Last night she wondered if it would become a hiding place in the future.

The evening seemed to go on forever, waiting for Grant to call or come home. She remembered how tired she felt as she looked out from the stately windows of the library and down onto the sandy moonlit beach of Springfield Lake. The view was picturesque compared to the carnage she had witnessed on the television screen. The sound of waves washing gently over the shoreline rocks produced an imitation peace at best. She was safe in this tranquil spot on earth, but there was no promise of safety in the future.

SHE KEPT DRIVING FARTHER INTO Dearborn, half-listening to Maggie while pondering her thoughts. Last evening was vividly sketched in her mind, even the trip to the kitchen for a late bite to eat. The light over the granite island eased the darkness of the approaching night. She glanced toward the back staircase near the opposite end of the kitchen, which led to the third-floor servant quarters where Maggie and Lillian lived. She wondered how late they would stay in nearby Toledo. Usually, she was happy they were out having fun and enjoying a day off, but tonight she wanted them here. Hungry and weary, she poured herself a glass of milk and opened a box of saltine crackers. She found the peanut butter in the pantry. Propping herself against the island counter, she drank the cold milk and nibbled the crackers, wishing Grant would call.

Feeling a little better, she returned to the library and took the Mission Plan from the file and placed it on the desk. She and Grant had spelled out step-by-step what should be done in the event of a threatening war. Instinctively she knew the plan would become a reality soon. Assuming that Grant was in a marathon meeting, she turned off the lights and left the room. For just a sharp moment, she felt confident that he would wake her when he arrived at the mansion or would call when he got to the condo in Dearborn.

Passing the solarium on the way to the massive staircase that led to several bedrooms upstairs, she turned and glanced at the plants, noticing how illuminated they were in the light of a full moon. The blossoms of the Himalayan Poppy looked magnificently translucent, and the leaves on the prized African violets looked as though they were growing fuzzy whiskers. Every plant in the round glass room was thriving. *Strange,* she thought to herself, *how quiet and beautiful the plants are, and how they are neither panicked nor plunged into a state of hysteria. How lucky they are to know nothing but to grow and be beautiful.*

She walked into the grand entrance hall, noticing the loud clicking of her shoes on the marble floor. Fear was gripping her spirit, but she dimmed the crystal chandelier and walked directly to the security key box at the right of the double mahogany front doors. With a trembling hand, she armed it and then turned in the direction of the grand room and called to her Cocker Spaniel, Duke, coaxing him to follow her up the staircase. Leaping the stairs ahead of her, he quickly found his place at the foot of her bed.

Beautiful pairs of sheer blue draperies elegantly flanked the sides of the wide windows in the master bedroom suite. They contrasted well with the white carpet and gave the bedroom an air of graceful good taste. Her canopy bed was the focal point of the room, with its white lace stretching over the high bedposts. A yellow and blue print spread generously dropped over the sides of the bed, crimping elegantly on the white carpet. The room was very vogue, very much like her.

The grandfather clock downstairs struck the hour. It was ten o'clock. She took off her clothes and put on a soft, cashmere nightshirt. Too tired and troubled to even brush her teeth, she stood for a moment in front of the vanity mirror, staring at her tall slim body. She took a brush and ran it through her long black hair, noticing that her face had all the fine features of her beautiful mother. She sighed, breathing aloud the word *Mother*.

Duke seemed a bit nervous, no doubt from sensing her anxiousness. She patted his head, turned down the spread, and dimmed the bedside lamp, easing into the silk sheets. Looking up through the transom windows, she saw hundreds of twinkling stars from galaxies far removed from her troubled world. Vividly aware that there would be other nights full of anxiety and fear, she closed her eyes and wished Grant was there beside her.

******

Now turning the corner on Miller Street, the condo came into Rachael and Maggie's view. Their hearts began beating like drums. Rachael pushed the garage door opener on the visor overhead. The door opened, and she saw Grant's car parked inside.

"Oh, thank God, he's here," Rachael cried.

In a flash, while Maggie was still fumbling her way out of the car, she ran into the garage. The moment of aroused gratitude lasted but a fraction of a second as she saw the slumped figure inside the car, leaning against the steering wheel. Grant's blood-soaked hair told the gruesome tale that he had been executed. His body was cold and gray.

Immediately her life seemed to end, right there on the garage cement floor. Her spirit moved into a black hole of despair. This could not be reality, yet she was incarcerated in it. It was a grip that had no pity. Stark, cold, and like nothing she had ever felt before she stood there, staring at Grant's body, with Maggie at her side weeping as though her heart would break. Rachael's knees buckled, and her eyes closed as she crumbled onto the garage floor.

******

As though a black abyss had swallowed her up, the struggle to manage the grief of Grant's murder was unbearable. His death created a void that dropped itself like a heavy boulder, crushing every ounce of life out of her. There was not a shred of convicting evidence that could tie Archer to the murder. Yet Rachael knew the bullet that killed her husband came from the gun of one of his cronies.

The memorial service allowed a measure of closure, but it was more like something operating by a gauge that only goes so far and then stops. Grant's death had solidified in Rachael and Maggie's minds that a one-world dictatorship was closer than ever, and they had work to do. All their past private conversations seemed accurate, perhaps more vivid and alive even without Grant's voice. There would be others that would die like him. People would conform or suffer the consequences.

THE MORBID QUIET AT THE mansion was viciously forcing reality that Grant was dead, while at the same time God's Spirit was speaking, nudging her to abandon her desire to wallow in sorrow. Beyond her human rationale, she seemed wrapped in a mystical awareness that Grant knew evil would touch her life, and he would not be there to help. He warned that things would get tough and admonished her that if anything happened to him, she was to keep pressing on.

She looked out from the huge grand room windows toward Springfield Lake, feeling empty, except for the heavy blanket of gloom encircling her spirit. To a stranger, the view of the lake would be pleasant, even breath-taking, but to Rachael, it was ineffectual. Her identity seemed obscure now that she was alone. The God she loved seemed lightyears away, as though tending to a galaxy that had more priority than the world she was being forced to survive in. She tried to choke back the tears that wanted to pour from her soul, but they came like a torrent, wanting to wash away all the sorrow. She threw herself on the sofa and wept.

It would take time, but Rachael would come to the understanding that evil is powerless, and this knowledge puts things in proper perspective. Although evil often accomplishes its goal, it remains in a powerless state within the control of God's purpose. One only needs to think of Hitler and understand his end and see in his evil act that the future of Israel's remnant was protected by God for decades to come.

"I need Your help, Lord," Rachael sobbed.

CHAPTER 2
THE UNSUSPECTED GIFT

SORROW BRUTALLY HOARDED RACHAEL AND kept her from the mission plan, even while knowing full well it had to be implemented without delay. Day and night she whirled around in a black pit of grief that made everything seem overwhelming. Getting out of bed each morning was a giant step. Maggie's warm compassion was appreciated, but the faithful maid could not heal her broken heart.

The mastermind invention at Holton Computer Corporation was sold to The Great Ten Nations, and in no time social media was buzzing with wonder and excitement. Real news and fake news was all over Facebook. Twitter was lit up like a Christmas tree. Newspaper articles and television reports across the globe were applauding the new financial system and reporting that The Great Ten Nations would start implementing it as soon as Holton released it into the hands of every world leader.

Rachael's Mission Plan needed immediate execution if she were to go forward with everything planned. The plan called for enormous work, all of which had to be followed systematically to the letter. But the daunting questions that hung in the balance plagued her emotions, causing her to wonder if she could regain her lost spirit and proceed without Grant. Would Maggie's help and support be sufficient?

Slowly pulling the leather office chair out from the desk, she sat down and thumbed through the stacked papers, finding the Mission Plan. Emotion heaved within her gut, and tears fell onto the papers making tiny wrinkled circles that seemed to symbolize the passion and fear her heart was experiencing. Each salty droplet was invisible ink, the ink of love, the ink of fear, both carrying a message to God and Grant. She picked the plan up and held the document close to her heart.

"Oh, Grant, I don't know how I'm going to do this without you, but somehow I must."

******

It would take months to implement the Mission Plan, so it was imperative that she start procedures to liquidate her assets in order to hold onto her wealth. The first line of business would be to sell the Carson Real Estate Corporation in New York City. If she neglected this important step, the firm would eventually become a ward of the new world regime.

The plan was precise. She would take as much cash from the sale of the corporation as was analytically possible, just enough to keep her lawyers' questions and curiosity at a manageable level. The cash would be placed into several new bank accounts at low amounts to keep the government's eyes off. It would be spent on the many essentials in the Plan, including a food bank and emergency supplies. The spacious mansion basement would hold the overflow of goods. She would also invest some of the money in stocks, which could be sold after her lawyers were out of the picture. All of this business needed to move rapidly. The concept behind the Plan was to liquidate the estate without notice before the worldwide system was fully activated. The mansion would be the only piece of property she would hold. It was debt-free, and she could pay the taxes years in advance.

It would break her heart, but the horses would be sold, and the stables closed down. She would also vacate the headquarters of Carson Real Estate office and the penthouse apartment in New York City. It seemed she was undergoing a surgical operation without the help of an anesthesiologist pouring pain killer into her veins. How could she sell almost everything that made up her life and survive the drastic change? Maggie was the only one left to her, and Lillian was just an employee who watched all this commotion with dim-witted sighs.

Somehow, within the human spirit, there is a phenomenal capacity to manage change, and Rachael began experiencing this phenomenon as she started the furious work. She was as focused as a cat sneaking toward a canary perched on a low tree limb.

Since the skies would be closely monitored with drones, it was imperative that Carson Hill undergo all the changes quickly. The world-wide cashless money exchanges would soon be in operation. Goods needed to be bought and hustled into the mansion pronto. From the very inception of this idea to create an emergency rescue mission, Rachael and Grant anticipated purchasing a van to transport victims out of dangerous situations and into safety. With this in mind, Rachael made immediate plans to purchase a new van and have it transported to the mansion by trailer. The delivery procedure of using a trailer would eliminate any insurance and licensing that could later be traced back to her. Although her request to transport the van by trailer seemed queer to the dealership, money was still good and hers was talking fast.

Grant included in the Mission Plan the name and phone number of a person who would issue her an assumed license plate and number, along with implied proofs of insurance. By doing this, her vehicle would never belong to the government. Hopefully, her implied proof of insurance would get her off the hook if she were stopped by a police officer, that is, if he would simply glance at her license and proof of insurance and let her go.

Her next move in the Plan was to set up escrow accounts with the utility companies to eliminate electronic monthly payments made to the bedeviled one-world economic system. Under the laws of the newfangled economic system, all debts, including mortgages, rent, and utilities, would be paid by computer by using a number assigned to the individual by the government. Rachael's smart decision to eliminate all contact with the new world financial system was not irrational or excessive by any means. She had a clear picture of the dire consequences of using this system, and she and Grant knew that the infrastructure of the system would not stop at merely owning every individual's wealth but would eventually demand the deification and worship of a world leader. So escrow accounts were paramount to remaining free. In the event the escrow plans failed, a generator and an underground gas tank would keep the mission running. Digging for the tank began immediately.

It became apparent while Grant was still alive, that bartering would eventually become a common practice throughout the country, as people secretly competed with one another to buy restricted merchandise or gain back lost possessions. Gems and fine jewelry would buy most anything in a world gone mad with class unification and economic hardship. Therefore, as soon as Rachael had the Mission Plan well underway, she set out to buy several pieces of fine jewelry, including diamond bracelets, gold chains, bracelets, and expensive watches for bartering purposes.

******

The Mediterranean war, and its clean-up, lasted long enough to get all affairs in order and complete the execution of the Plan. The real estate business sold immediately to a large investment company in Texas. The other assets, though not moving on the market as quickly, were negotiated in good time. Meanwhile, The Great Ten Nations were moving swiftly to achieve their bullish objectives and get the world moving in line with the coalition's agenda. Holton Computer Corporation continued to make newspaper headlines around the globe. World leaders referred to their outstanding achievement as their answer to solving everything from the troubling stock markets to the elimination of gross fraud and collusion. The software was being manufactured in the US and Japan for immediate installation on all business networks, including banks. Like a well-oiled machine, everything was moving fast, and the masses were duped into believing this was the greatest plan man had ever created.

******

Maggie and Lillian begin to arrange the bedrooms for occupancy of hungry defecting Americans, those innocent and unyielding citizens who, by their faith, would refuse the tyranny of the new world regime and subsequently be destined to suffer the loss of everything they owned. Insubordination to the government would be quickly consequential. For most people, the lack of foreknowledge to see the approaching tyranny would cause them persecution. In one fail swoop, the government would reap grave consequences upon everyone in the US and throughout the world if they failed to comply.

Maggie and Lillian's work needed to get finished quickly. They stepped to a faster pace when Rachael received word that an underground network of patriotic citizens based out of Troy, Michigan was secretly organizing in small groups throughout the country to help the victims of the new world order. Each patriot in these secret groups worked as a partner in liberty, to help rescue those in imminent danger for refusing to bend their knee to the emerging fascism. Rachael had little information about these groups but felt comforted by the thought that she was not alone in this crude fight for freedom. Poor homeless victims would soon be coming to her mansion.

As soon as every State Department became centralized and local businesses were hooked into the system, the mansion would become a busy place. Some individuals might need medical care when they arrived. Deeply concerned, Rachael sent word to the secret underground in Troy for medical supplies. She requested common prescription drugs, even hoping for a doctor, or at least a nurse.

******

Life was far from what it was in the Carson Real Estate Corporation. There were no elaborate social dinners, lucrative business contracts, or trips between New York and Michigan. Instead, Rachael spent hours on the phone and on the road contracting and buying what was required to get the mission ready. The gas tank and pump were installed, and the new generator was fed to the gas line, ready if needed in the future. Escrow accounts were set up with the utility companies with monies that gave the mansion several years without requiring the world system. Maggie and Lillian were working feverishly to pack every cabinet and closet with survival provisions, including blankets, sheets, pillows, towels, and toiletries. Food supplies were stocked in the kitchen pantries and on new shelves in the mammoth basement. Lillian, who served as cook and culinary expert, reluctantly resigned herself to going along with the Plan. She surrendered, not because she was convinced that tyranny would rule the world, but because she needed a job and a place to live. Underneath her guarded façade, she loved Rachael, so staying was more than being a good sport, and it was no small note that her help was more than coveted due to her knowledge of food preparation and quantities needed. Her careful attention to stocking all sorts of foods, both canned and packaged, was resourceful. Her suggestions to buy cases of canned beans, meat, fish, fried rice, chili, spaghetti, stew, fruits, and fruit juices, along with vegetables and jars of spaghetti sauce, plus pounds of pasta and rice were as good as any dietician could offer. The mansion was stocked like a huge hospital. Lillian was a genius in this area.

She took Maggie with her to a wholesale conglomerate and bought copious boxes of biscuit flour, knowing that this enriched flour could create cakes, muffins, and pancakes. She arranged to have two new upright freezers brought into the basement to keep flour, dried milk, butter, and select cheeses fresh for months. Canned goods and staples like sugar, coffee, coffee creamer, powdered milk, tea, along with bottles of fruit drinks, cooking oil, and nuts of all sorts, were stored on the new basement shelves and in boxes that lined the basement walls.

The maids worked like a professional team and wisely shopped at different markets outside the area, so as not to create curiosity by their massive purchases. Rachael calculated that their storehouse could feed about fifteen people for several months without resorting to the practice of bartering.

THE UNDERGROUND NETWORK TOOK RACHAEL'S request seriously. Their response assured her that she would receive medical supplies, including antiseptics, analgesics, and antibiotics. All this was made possible by a wealthy doctor, nicknamed Luke, a Jewish professional who had converted to Christianity many years ago. He would arrange to have the supplies delivered to the mansion from his office in Farmington Hills. The journey to transport these items would require a two-hour drive to the Irish Hills during which extreme precautions would be put in place.

******

It was several weeks after getting word that medical supplies would be brought to Carson Hill when a van carrying the precious cargo pulled up to the servant's entrance at the back of the mansion. Rachael peeked through the kitchen window to get a look at the delivery man and thought it strange that he was dressed in what appeared to be great-looking designer jeans and a sport coat. His dark brown hair reached his collar, and his eyes were bright and happy. She guessed his age at late thirties, maybe early forties.

"Are you Rachael Garrison?" the man asked, standing at the doorway with one of the medicine crates in his arms.

"Yes, and you must be from Dr. Luke," Rachael replied, motioning for him to come into the kitchen.

He nodded and entered, looking quickly around to find a place to set the heavy crate.

"You can put the crates here, on the island counter," she told him.

There were fifteen crates inconspicuously packed in boxes neatly secured with strapping tape. All of them fictitiously labeled as office supplies in the event the van was stopped and searched.

"I've cleared out a large walk-in closet in the game room on the second floor for medical supplies," she told the man. "We can use the service elevator to take the crates up. By the way, I don't know your name."

The man turned to her. "I'm Kendall Saunders, Dr. Luke's son.

"Oh, then your father's last name is Saunders," Rachael commented, shaking hands enthusiastically.

"Yes, but for all security purposes, he must be referred to as Dr. Luke."

"Of course," she said, understanding that she now lived in a world of intrigue and secrecy.

It took only a few minutes to get the medical supplies onto the elevator. Kendall was impressed with the mission operation and how well it appeared to be organized.

"Let me take you through the mansion and show you what we have done," she said, as they put the last of the crates onto the shelves.

With a great sense of accomplishment, she took him into every room on the second floor, showing him how she, and her staff of two, had set each room up to accommodate the people the underground in Troy would send to her.

"This room can accommodate a family of eight," she said, as she took him into the rearranged master suite.

"God forbid if it should happen, but we have enough bedroom space in this place to quarantine those who get sick," she said. "I've tried to think of everything."

There was plenty of room all right, but Kendall was not so much interested in quarantines as he was her, noticing how pretty she was and what beautiful eyes she had. He also saw a woman of great courage and deep spiritual complexity, someone who was definitely on a mission ordained by God.

"One thing you might want to do, Rachael," he commented, "is to buy a medical examining table. In the event minor surgeries are needed, a sturdy table would be a necessity."

"Oh, I never thought of that, but it's a good idea if, of course, if we ever have a doctor working with us."

They walked down the winding staircase into the entrance hall and then into the grand room. Kendall was impressed with the elegance of this beautiful place, the paintings and the tapestries, the plants in the solarium, the exquisite furniture, the expensive rugs, all of it exhibited taste and refined class. It was nothing like he had imagined. Nor was Rachael anything like he thought he might encounter. He figured someone much older and perhaps a bit matronly, such as an elderly angel of mercy.

"I've left everything unchanged on the first floor so if the authorities show up unexpectedly, they will not suspect I'm running a rescue mission," she told him. "I plan to train everyone who takes refuge here to quickly get out of sight when a knock comes at the door."

Kendall was completely astonished at how well thought out everything was, and how ready Carson Hill was to take in the poor indigent victims of the new world order.

"What about upstairs?" he asked. "You cannot hide the medical supplies and the large amounts of bedding and towels. A search upstairs would surely clue authorities that you are hiding people."

"Yes," she answered, "but that's where faith comes in. I can't hide everything, so I must trust God."

Kendall understood her optimism and fully appreciated her faith, but somehow he could not imagine the government avoiding a search of the entire mansion if they got wind of her mission.

THEY VENTURED TO THE BASEMENT where Kendall observed the elaborate wine cellar and commented on it being a perfect hiding place in the event the mission was found out. He was impressed with the amount of frozen food in the freezers and stacked shelves of every canned and packaged food imaginable. Even more was his fascination with the gasoline pump outside and the generator. It seemed to him that every possible thing that would be needed to run a mission of mercy had been thought of and completely covered.

"This had to take a lot of thought and a lot of inspiration to accomplish," he said. "I can only imagine the financial sacrifice."

"Yes, but I know this is what I should do," she replied, not allowing any expression of forfeit or loss. "It's just more difficult because my husband is not here to help me."

Kendall noticed a sudden sorrow in her voice. He knew the reason. His father informed him about Grant's murder and told him that Grant died trying to thwart the computer software that was now being implemented worldwide. He was told that no one would be prosecuted for Grant's death. He wondered if revenge was incubating in her heart. If so, he could not see it. Maybe she had given it over to God, but sorrow was in her voice.

"This mission is an exhausting task," he said, while they walked up the basement stairs and into the kitchen. Rachael motioned for him to take a seat at the table.

THERE WAS A CONVENIENT LULL in their conversation that gave Kendall an opportunity to mention his Jewish grandfather and how his parents made their way to America.

"My grandfather died in a Nazi concentration camp, without food or medical attention," he said. "If there had been something like this mission accessible to him, he might not have suffered.

"My father was just a young boy of twelve when the German's dragged my grandparents out of their home and took them to the camps. My father was not home at the time, which was a miracle because from that point on, he managed to stay hidden until the war was over."

How ironic it seemed to all of them that the world was going backward, grabbing hold again of the days when many countries and millions of people hid from tyranny during World War II. Rachael listened with interest and motioned for Lillian to pour coffee and set a plate of banana bread on the table. She didn't want to interrupt Kendall for one moment because she felt the suffering of this man's grandparents. Her connection came easy considering that her husband's body lay buried in a grave because of evildoers.

Kendall kept talking and took a slice of the bread. He buttered it while he told them the rest of the story. "America was good to my father. Getting here was a difficult voyage, but once he got here, he worked hard and received his doctorate through incredible opportunities."

Rachael couldn't help but wonder if God had not saved Kendall's father for just a time as this, but she kept the thought to herself.

"I can't tell you how sad he is about the new government faction coming on the scene," Kendall continued. "He knows firsthand what fascist rule can bring, and that is why he wants to help you. He wants this mission to work well, to keep operating and save lives."

His words burned deep into her heart, and thankfulness overflowed. The Saunders' support was more than hoped for. She had no medical background but knew that the supplies and antibiotics Kendall delivered would comfort many lives, especially the children who would come with fevers and stomach aches. Still, she wished for a doctor or even a nurse to help in the mission.

Sitting in the kitchen sipping coffee together and talking about human suffering seemed to bring a sense of solidarity between them. Although there was a strong element of concern for their futures, there was also reassurance that whatever was ahead would not be faced alone. Many Christians were uniting, and that was a comforting component within their unknown futures.

Maggie was listening and nodding her head at most of the conversation. Years of life experiences and her knowledge of End Time prophecy emboldened her to encourage both of them to keep their perspectives focused and their hopes centered on faith and trust.

"You young folks must keep up your courage," she said. "God is in all of what is happening, and He has got the final word. Many will be hiding in small groups. The enemy will never be able to find all of them. God always makes sure there is a surviving remnant of Believers."

This was Maggie the patriot talking. As for Lillian, her sweat equity in the mission plan was bringing her slowly into considering that what was taking place before her eyes was incredible enough to almost believe.

"The time will come when we may have to die for what we believe," Kendall said rather soberly.

That was all Lillian needed to hear to strike up her ceaseless skepticism. She shrugged her shoulders, doubting she would ever become a martyr. But for Maggie, it was not a matter of ambivalence or doubt. She knew that what was about to come upon the scene would vex her very soul and possibility number her among the martyrs. Her greatest concern was for Rachael, the child God gave her for her very own when Catherine died.

"IT'S TIME I STARTED BACK," Kendall said, as he reached into his pocket and pushed a business card into Rachael's hand.

"This card has my cell number on it," he said. "I am a doctor like my dad, and I want you to call me when you have ill people here. I'll come whenever you need me."

Tears came to Rachael's eyes as she realized that this was the one detail in the plan that had not been met until now. She looked at the business card and slid her thumb over the embossed letters of Kendall's printed name, feeling as though he was sent by God.

"Wow!" she said as if that was the only word that would come to her after such a surprise. "This is wonderful, I mean, an answer to prayer. Thank you so much."

She hugged him.

Maggie stood there, wiping her eyes with the apron tied around her waist and mumbled quietly, "Thank you, Jesus."

Watching the van leave, the three women waited on the driveway until it was no longer in sight before walking back into the mansion. The scene of him driving away felt like a farewell to family, like parents might feel when their adult children have visited for a few hours and the house is quiet and lonely again. Rachael thought of how good it was to have a man visit the house and to offer to help whenever a medical situation occurred and perhaps do other things they could not do.

There was more work to be done, but the burden seemed lighter knowing they had a committed medical person on board.

******

A cold gray sky spread across Springfield Lake and over Carson Hill, hinting that winter had arrived. Through the tall transom windows of the grand room, Rachael watched the clouds release snowflakes fluttering deftly to the ground and making Carson Hill divinely serene, as though it existed somewhere else, rather than in a world that would soon be suffering tyranny on a scale never known before to mankind. She stretched her body across the white brocade sectional, relaxing her anxious mind, if that were possible. Duke nestled close, his warm furry body resting near her head. Gently she smoothed his fur while her mind moved to a time when life was full of happiness and excitement. She missed Grant. The thought of him moved her memory into a world she once loved and a time when life was filled with ecstasy . . .

THROUGHOUT THE EVENING, GRANT HAD been the perfect host at their penthouse apartment in New York. Their clients, David Palmer and Foster Manus, were dinner guests. The evening was spent in an effort to encourage Palmer and Manus to arrange for their company lawyers to set up a deal with another compatible company they were planning to merge with. The business clients were seriously looking at integrating their two multi-million-dollar manufacturing industries into one large conglomerate. The merger would involve purchasing a local land site for their headquarters, and that's where Carson Real Estate Corporation came into play.

Rachael watched Grant's smooth style, knowing that he wanted this deal very much, but was disciplining his anxious impulses to remain patient and play the game with savvy clout. Occasionally he would wink at her when Palmer and Manus were not looking, exercising the intimacy they shared.

Grant at all times garnered a business-like manner while at the same time modeling gracious social *savoir-faire*. The dinner menu Rachael chose was not too upper crust, just expensive enough to set the atmosphere that Palmer and Manus would feel exclusive. Lillian presented the meal beautifully. The evening was as perfect as one could hope for, with Rachael performing as the executive owner of the firm, supported by Grant who was covertly dazzling her with his handsome shrewdness.

In their bedroom, after the deal was solidified and the clients gone, Rachael waited for Grant's touch. Her love for him went deep, not because he was handsome and clever, but because of the man inside. He was honest yet cautiously cunning. He was strong, yet gentle and kind. He was her enchanted knight who had come into her life to sweep her into the realm of adoration and irresistible devotion. Above all, they shared a common faith in Jesus Christ.

She sat on the edge of the bed, watching him unbutton his shirt and pull it off his masculine shoulders. He threw the shirt onto the bench at the foot of the bed and caught her eyes watching him. A cunning smile swept across his face. He moved toward her, reaching out his arms and gently pulling her up from the bed and into an embrace. His arms always shut out the world, as though nothing existed but their love for each other. He tilted his head to look at her for a moment and then gently kissed her.

******

Snow covered Carson Hill, wrapping it in a white blanket of soft fluff that looked far too beautiful to be disturbed by the noisy plows scraping the road around Springfield Lake. Maggie walked into the grand room with a tray of fresh sliced fruit, sweet shortbread cookies, and a pot of steaming Earl Grey tea.

"I brought some tea and goodies for you," she said to Rachael, while carefully setting the tray on the ottoman in front of the plush sectional.

"You worry me, child," she continued. "You're not resting and eating like you should."

"Oh, Maggie, I'm okay," Rachael responded, straightening up so she could pour a cup of the hot tea.

"Sit with me a while; I need some company." She patted the cushion next to her and shoved Duke out of the way.

As if they both realized that time was closing in on their leisure and their conversations would soon change and be lost in the grind of daily mission work, they relished this moment together. All too soon, sipping tea would be replaced by common meals with strangers. The quiet atmosphere of the mansion would cease, giving place to clatter and routine work.

CHAPTER 3

CHIMERA

THE WORLD WAS NAIVELY DUPED with Holton Corporation's one-world system of global commerce. Rachael viewed the madness as a form of coherent delirium. The daily news coming over the wires was dreadful. It depicted a world gone mad, and it caused her flesh to crawl every time she stopped to listen. The masses remained hoodwinked and ignorant of their doomed future. Most nights Rachael could not sleep. Her mind was always working—always traveling back into the past or projecting into the future. Tonight was no different. Her mind conjured up an old movie she watched during her college years. It was a passé classic of the life story of the late Reverend Peter Marshall, Chaplain of the US Senate during the late nineteen forties. *He was my father's age,* she thought to herself, remembering that he became Chaplain of the Senate just four years after World War II ended. The storyline of this famous Presbyterian minister was characterized beautifully in his chronicle, "A Man Called Peter," written by his devoted wife, Catherine. For some weird reason, this outdated movie was haunting Rachael's memory.

The story depicted a man of great nobleness, but yet a bit of a romantic. He came to America from Scotland, carrying with him an ordained call into Protestant ministry. Arriving in America, he found a land that appreciated his spiritual genius and a people who wanted to hear what he had to say. Some were willing to wait in long lines to hear him preach.

In her mind's eye, she remembered a scene from the old movie. How ironic that she was remembering it fifteen years after first viewing it during her college years as part of an assignment. Peter Marshall had just accepted the position of Chaplain of the Senate and arrived with his wife in Washington, DC, from New York City. He had stars in his eyes while he stood outside the Capitol Building. Looking up at the massive structure and sensing the power that it held within, he turned to Catherine and told her how much he loved this place. There was a lot wrong with it, but it still had a lot right. He told her he could feel the nation's heartbeat, the pulse of liberty, liberty for the whole world.

It seemed to Rachael that Peter Marshall's America was now a beaten Republic and a perfect picture of *Mystery Babylon*, ready for judgment. His beloved land was headed for internal destruction, and she was convinced when people finally recognized the new system as a crafty delusion, they would rebel. Reality would hit hard, exposing the world leaders' evil ideology, which would bring mutiny. *Old Grandpa Carson was right*, Rachael thought. *It's only a matter of time before the Red Horse of Destruction rides through the world.*

She sat down on the burgundy leather couch in the library, lowering her shoulders to rest her elbows on her lap and put her face into her hands. Maggie and Lillian were in their quarters upstairs sleeping. The mansion was quiet, but the burden upon her shoulders screamed loud and felt weighty, as if the world rested solely upon her. How unfair it seemed that only a few people knew the truth. Her thoughts reeled. One tear and then another slipped from her eyes, and before she could gain control, she was weeping as though her heart had been ripped from her chest. Indeed, it was midnight for the nations, and the appointment with kismet had arrived.

******

Instead of approaching the one-world system of The Great Ten Nations with cautious reluctance, the masses continued applauding the beastly invention. In ignorance they saw the plan as a marvelous economic intercession that promised them liberty and peace beyond their wildest imaginations. They thought their safety was secure. Terrorist attacks would stop. Money would jingle in their pockets. All would be well. The foreshadowing of the new world order was promising euphoria in their duped minds.

GERMANY IMPLEMENTED THE MASSIVE COMPUTER operation with speed and great success. Appropriately, the system was named Chimera, meaning fantasy, but its true meaning was reaching far beyond a castle in the sky. The remnant of Christians throughout the world viewed this invention as a pure fabrication of peace. Reports on social media were that many had been killed because of their insubordination. This entire set-up was a delusion, rapidly working its way through Europe like a wild, whimsical hallucination that had risen to life by the breath of covetous evildoers.

Throngs of people were flocking to the authorities, getting the iris of their eyes scanned and being processed into a personal identification classification with a 15-digit number. That number was stored immediately in the master computers worldwide. To complete the process, a computer chip was placed under their skin on the left forehand with the same identification number. In the United States, the scene was the same. Lines formed in an orderly fashion while people received their numbers. Watching the news coverage was nauseating because it looked like animals being tagged for slaughter.

Archer's computer software made him rich and famous. The mastermind of this colossal plan was revered for his brilliant invention. His clever subordinates—those computer wizards who worked feverishly to create his brainchild—were presently scattered in major cities overseas, assisting the authorities in adopting the system. The success of the program throughout all the world was on the heels of complete implementation.

Chimera was being enforced in the US as fast as the software could be installed across the nation. Businesses and corporations, regardless of size, were ordered to comply within ninety days. Individual concurrence was expected of every person, both for buying and selling. Everyone was advised to install a home version of the software on their personal computers, and include scanners as part of the necessary equipment needed for buying and selling. The complete software package was made available at every post office, Secretary of State Office, and City Hall.

The consequences of not complying with the system were made crystal clear in a Presidential announcement on both radio and television. It was clearly understood that without compliance to Chimera, no buying or selling would be authorized. Groceries stores, department stores, doctor's offices, hospitals, banks, transportation terminals, utility companies, telephone companies, car dealerships, ticket offices, or private enterprise that beckoned a buyer or a seller, or offered a service of any kind was now requiring digital identification.

Cash, checks, debit cards, and charge cards were no longer valid tenders. Individual earnings were directly credited into the system from where the earning took place. Under every identification number, the person's earnings and net worth were recorded.

Rachael understood that the time of deep sorrow was at hand. Escaping from the new world system would require cautious bartering from here on when they needed something they did not have.

******

According to secret information from Dr. Luke's office in Troy, Michigan, underground operations were becoming widespread throughout the country. While the successful launch of the worldwide economic system proceeded, new Christian underground operations in the US continued to be secretly organized at phenomenal speed.

As the world was changing, no one went anywhere or did anything without hearing about the new economic system. Americans were reacting no differently than the Europeans. Like them, they were enthralled with the new system. From California to New York City, people were celebrating the new order as though it had been handed to them by the god of prosperity. And while they danced in the streets, without knowing that some people were being persecuted by the government, Rachael was keenly aware that it would only be a short time before Chimera became an ugly burgeoning beast, robbing individuals of their potential and making the world a common village.

THE UNDERGROUND NETWORK HEADQUARTERED IN Troy acquired the name of Bible Believer's Operation (BBO). Their office was one of many operating underground in Michigan, as well as hundreds operating throughout the US. Each had its own name. Christians were experiencing reality in the form of a dreadful threat to their faith and the survival of their families.

******

In the Grosse Pointe area of Detroit, Rose Garner, a seventy-five-year-old retired school teacher, became the first victim to be rescued by the BBO underground network. She had been ostracized for refusing to use Chimera and was barely surviving when BBO moved to help her. Presently, her possessions were spent, and she was poverty-stricken. Without warning, her utilities were shut off, and a repossession notice was issued on her house, in spite of the fact that she had no mortgage. It was astounding how fast Michigan unified itself with Washington's mandate and was exercising Chimera profitably—even to the point of confiscating personal property and punishing citizens who were not using the system out of their homes.

Rachael was informed by the BBO of the woman's need for a place to take refuge. For the time being, the poor woman was safe, finding refuge with kind neighbors. But she was to be transported to the Irish Hill's mansion quickly before the authorities learned of her whereabouts.

Rose was a model school teacher, graduating as an English major from the University of Michigan. She was a woman of elegance and intellect, all of which she had carried with her into the sacred halls of Vernier High School, located near the Civic Center in downtown Detroit, where she taught for over thirty years. She was the epitome of professionalism. Her grace invaded the classroom like a welcome breath of fresh air, and she demanded respect from every student.

Agile and independent for an older woman, Rose had been financially secure until now, with a monthly pension, stock investment dividends, and a Social Security check every month. Her honorable work in the public school system had been awarded time and time again. She held a seat on the Detroit City Council for many years and directed charitable organizations. The woman was a revered community member, but now shamefully reduced to nothing because she refused to adhere to the demands of Chimera.

She had definitely paid her dues to God and mankind, but instead of reaping the benefits of her lifelong labor, she found herself stonebroke and cast off. The deep convictions of her soul, those judgments of passion and conscience that kept her from embracing Chimera, held for her severe consequences that were more than she could survive under. Rachael was eager to bring her to the mansion.

Plans were quickly finalized for Rachael to drive to Gross Pointe. She would travel during the morning rush hour and drive with extreme caution so as not to attract attention to the van. If the van was spotted by the police for a traffic violation, the bogus license plate and registration might be found out, and that would mean imprisonment. It was crucial that she stay inconspicuous in traffic and drive carefully. Plans also included picking up the Hopkins family on the way back from Grosse Pointe. The family of four lived in Allen Park, a downriver community of Detroit, twenty-seven miles south of Grosse Pointe.

Paul and Karen Hopkins were temporarily taking refuge in a neighborhood church after losing their jobs, their cars, and eventually their house to the evil system. Paul worked as a linesman at the Ford Rouge Plant. He lost his job after refusing to comply with

Chimera's demands that were forced upon the company's payroll system. He refused to be screened and documented. He stubbornly would not be tossed into the heinous world system. But in no time, his paychecks stopped.

Karen likewise was fired from her position as a US postal worker after she refused to use the one-world operation. The BBO rushed their names to Rachael as soon as they learned of their crisis.

An early morning fog made driving out of the Irish Hills difficult. Rachael could hardly see twenty feet in front of the van as she pulled onto M-50 and headed east toward Detroit. Maggie was with her, silently keeping all her frightful thoughts to herself, while the wipers flopped back and forth, clearing the dense fog off the windshield. In the console between them was a map and the addresses of Rose Garner and the Hopkins family, which included two children, under ten years old, Stacey and Michael.

"It's like pea soup out here," Rachael said, keeping a strong grip on the steering wheel. Her voice was charged with anxiety. This being their first run for the mission, they were two vulnerable women starting out on a tricky trip that might prove to be a *mission impossible*. Successful completion of this run was of chief importance. If she was caught driving a vehicle without proper credentials, the whole operation would come to a halt.

"We'll be fine, Rachael," Maggie commented, although she was experiencing the same fear.

The low hum of the van's engine and the constant squeak of the wipers moving back and forth to clear the wet fog became the only sound breaking the silence. Daylight would break about the time Rachael pulled onto the Interstate, some forty-five miles ahead. The sun would help clear the thick fog. Keeping their eyes squarely on the short span of visible road in front of them, they drove steadily into the darkness.

ROSE WAS WATCHING FROM THE window as the van pulled up in front of the house. She had a sense of relief that her rescuers made the trip safely and found the house, but for Rachael the challenge of the long drive back was of deep concern.

"Come in with me, Maggie, and help with her things," Rachael said, shutting off the motor and opening the door. She stood outside the van for a moment, looking around, as if she might see someone watching.

As they walked up the sidewalk to the cement front porch, the door opened, and Rose reached out to welcome them. With tears in her eyes, she hugged and thanked them for coming. The elderly couple who befriended her stood in the background, hesitating in the dining room archway, just a few feet away. *Strange*, Rachael thought, *why are they shying back?*

The house seemed extremely small, probably because there was far too much furniture. On the walls were pictures hung so high they looked odd. Crocheted doilies were on the arms of the couch and under each lamp. Stretch-type slipcovers donned the chairs. The room depicted the early fifties era, and Rachael surmised that the couple was a bit eccentric, if not extremely odd. Obviously, they fancied what they owned and how they displayed it, even if it was outdated.

The air was stale and far too warm in the house. She caught the couple's kind eyes as they reluctantly moved forward to shake her hand. The scene was like a chapter out of a mystery thriller. Strangers meeting under extreme circumstances, and no one completely trusting the other. A mysterious but sacred sense of purpose was there, as though a providential guiding spirit was permeating the room, and Rachael sensed it as she shook hands with the elderly couple and tried to appear as a long-lost relative of Rose. Similar scenes like this would be played out again and again in the underground mission efforts throughout the country.

Standing there in this peculiar house, meeting this odd couple who loved doilies and high-hung pictures, and doing it for the purpose of rescuing a person from the throes of Chimera, spawned thundering excitement in Rachael's every nerve. All her life she had been intellectually and spiritually tutored for this moment in time. Maggie too. But neither of them could deny the intrinsic confirmation that was saturating their spirits, the assurance that the wisdom of God had brought them both to this moment in time. But just as one clap of thunder meets with another, Rachael had a troubling thought: *what if this kind-looking old couple was part of a spy operation?* No, the BBO would not send her into a spy net.

Rachael tried not to gape at Rose, but her charm and attractiveness were fascinating. The lady's silver hair was beautifully swept back into a French twist, showing off her pretty face that barely had a wrinkle. Her tall frame was elegant. She was dressed in an expensive navy blue suit. Her shoes were made of fine leather. She was every bit as classy and dignified as the BBO described.

"Here, let me help you with that," Maggie said, taking the woman's suitcase and helping her into the van.

Rachael turned to bid goodbye. The old man came close again to shake her hand.

She nearly jumped back in fear as she spied the tiny bulge on the left hand of the old man, indicating an implanted computer chip. Noticing her fear, the old man said, "It's okay, you're safe."

Immediately she knew what the situation was. The odd couple were indeed Christians, but they threw their allegiance to Chimera out of fear. *How many more Christians would do the same,* Rachael wondered. Her heart was saddened. *What does a choice like this mean to God?* These were questions she could not answer, but it opened up a whole new set of issues she had not thought about. What exactly is the allegiance to God in matters of life and death? Knowing the carefulness of the BBO, she was sure the old man was safe. But she was not sure how safe his soul was.

AS THE VAN HEADED FOR Allen Park, small chitchat helped break the ice. Rose was quite an impressive personality. She fascinated Rachael with her knowledge of the world system and its negative ramifications. For her, and many like her, the underground operations were the only salvation for those refusing to give allegiance to Chimera, but many had not prepared for it.

"People will die because of their loyalty to their convictions," the retired school teacher said. "There is no doubt that this evil thing will never be stopped."

Rachael nodded, glancing in her rear-view mirror at the traffic behind. The fog had given way to sunshine, but it was still rush hour, and driving continued to be challenging. She carefully negotiated the traffic and eased the van into the farthest right lane of the expressway, staying in the slow stream of moving vehicles. Spotting their exit to Allen Park, Maggie picked up the map and read the directions to the church.

PAUL HOPKINS WAS STANDING OUTSIDE, watching for them. As soon as he saw the van pulling into the parking lot, he turned and quickly opened the church door to gather his family outside. Each had a suitcase in hand, including his young children. Their pastor followed, carrying a large box in his arms. The scene was much like it was in Grosse Pointe, hurried and careful.

"We're so glad you made it safely," the pastor said, still holding onto Rachael's hand as he talked. "We've been praying for you all morning."

"Thanks, we have felt those prayers," she said, looking at Maggie for affirmation.

"Yes, indeed we have," Maggie spoke up while taking the small suitcase from the little girl, Stacey.

The children stood quiet and shy while the adults talked quickly. The moment seemed charged with a peculiar sense of strength and courage that wrapped itself around Rachael, much like what she felt at the home of the old odd couple. It seemed as though she had a legion of support, not only from the underground but also from the armies of heaven. She sensed from the pastor's words that there were hundreds of people in the Metropolitan Detroit Area who were standing firm against Chimera. Soon there would be countless victims needing help. Instinctively she knew that her mansion could never hold even a fraction of those in trouble. She reached down and patted Michael's head, speaking softly to both him and to his sister, hoping to distract them from fear. Paul and the pastor lifted the remaining suitcases into the van, while Karen and Maggie looked on.

Paul took the large box the pastor placed near the van and handed it to Rachael.

"This box is filled with toys and children's books. The ladies of the church also included some children's clothes. We felt you might be short on these things."

Rachael's smile swept broadly across her face. "Your impressions are right; we did not stock many of those items." She turned and hugged the pastor.

"We will be in touch with you as others come to us," he said. "God's speed on your way back."

******

Lillian had soup and sandwiches ready when the van arrived at the mansion. Everyone gathered in the kitchen at the large breakfast table, a cozier place to eat and talk, rather than sitting in the formal dining room. With stomachs full and everyone feeling more relaxed, Rachael showed her new residents around the mansion. With confidence fully regained from the long trip into the challenging Metro Detroit area, and feeling self-assured about her mission, she expressed to the new residents the importance of abiding by the rules and regulations set up to keep the mission running smoothly.

Breakfast would be served each morning at eight o'clock, lunch at twelve-thirty, and dinner at six. She emphasized that each adult would have duties. Children would have specific times for studies and play. In the event of an unexpected knock at the door, all personal paraphernalia would be immediately hidden out of sight, and everyone would hurry into the wine cellar if they were on the first floor. Rachael and her staff would handle immediate situations should anyone come to the mansion unannounced. Residents were to be ready at all times to move quickly out of sight.

Snacking or drinking would not be allowed outside the kitchen. No visible clues would be left for the authorities to suspect residents. Practice drills to keep them accustomed to getting out of sight would take place periodically. On Sunday morning, breakfast would be served an hour later to allow additional rest. Everyone would then gather in the grand room at ten o'clock for worship and singing. A copy of the rules was handed to them for reference.

"Two things I want to stress," Rachael said as she took them upstairs to assign bedrooms. "First, keep your personal items out of sight in your rooms in the event authorities enter the mansion and search the upstairs. If you have time and can get to the cellar, run quickly. Otherwise, do the best you can.

"Second," she went on, "bathing is expected every day unless you are ill. Clean clothes are a must. Shoes and shirts are expected to be worn at every meal, along with using good table manners. We are a family now, and consideration of each person's rights and feelings are expected."

She turned to glance at her new residents as she talked, noticing that the three adults were in agreement. This speech would be given again and again as new residents came to the mansion.

The Hopkins family was given a bedroom with three beds and a private bath. Rose was given a bedroom with two double beds, and would be sharing her room should another single woman come to the mansion.

"Laundry days will be assigned by Maggie tomorrow," Rachael concluded.

PHYSICALLY AND MENTALLY EXHAUSTED FROM the day's activities, Rachael lingered under the warm water of the shower before donning pajamas. Thankful for the accomplishments of the day, she relaxed in a comfy overstuffed chair near the fireplace, one of many fireplaces throughout the mansion—all converted to gas flames years ago. This was not her bedroom, but one she chose for herself to save the master suite for a large family.

She sat for a few minutes, thinking how peculiar everything was. The rules and regulations were turning the mansion into a place so different it seemed strange. Nothing was like life used to be with Grant. She couldn't help feeling like a stranger in her own home.

Soft light emitting from the Tiffany floor lamp near a small round table dimly defined her journal. She picked it up and thumbed through to find the next blank page to write about today:

October 30. Today has been my most exhausting and gratifying day yet. Asleep in two of the mansion's bedrooms are victims of the evildoers, casualties of Chimera. They sleep with full stomachs tonight, safe in clean, warm beds. Tonight, more than ever before in my life, I am assured of my high calling to save victims of despair and to show the love of God. I know if Grant is looking on at this moment, he is well pleased.

CHAPTER 4

GIVE ME THE POOR, THE REJECTED REFUGEES

TYRANNY IN THE US WAS now the main issue for conscientious American citizens. The subject was not a drifting topic, but an actual situation. All nations and kingdoms were now living under the threat of a misrepresented political system, although most had not fully realized their loss of freedom and diminishing individual wealth. Mainstream media reports were projecting that it would take about three and one-half years to completely implement the Chimera system and get world-wide commerce running smoothly. In every country of the world, individuals were being forced into wealth distribution. To the poor and lower class, the new assessment meant little in terms of lost materialism, but to the middle class and beyond, it boiled down to future capital becoming government-owned revenue. The rich and the famous were enraged, yet they passively rescinded after being assured that Chimera would allow them to keep the assets they had already accumulated. Just how unfair the process would end up becoming was not known, but one thing seemed certain to Rachael, the leaders of The Great Ten Nations would fill their pockets and salivate for more and more power. Worldwide complacency would eventually lead to anarchy. When people realized they had been duped into a plan that stole their desire for advancement and their enthusiasm to excel, hatred would justify lawlessness.

Under the tenets of Chimera's rule, Rachael's mission was becoming more vital to those who would refuse to obey.

FOOD AND MISCELLANEOUS SUPPLIES AT the mansion were holding out well, but the effects of Chimera was merely in the beginning stage. Lillian deliberated and carefully weighed each day's rations, working diligently to conserve food, yet serve nutritious meals. For the time being, the residents had no qualms about their meals or abiding by strict rules. Could they dare to be any other way? The conscious reminder of their miraculous rescue allowed them to be happy for bread and water if that was all they could get. How long this appreciative attitude would last was unknown. Each individual was dealing with their losses and fears. They were hurting while also forcing encouraging talk and support toward one another to soften their wounds.

When spirits were low, smiles were plastic. On occasion, the concealed panic, inner fears, and morbid depression of isolation were outweighed only by *the will to live.* The residents of Rachael's mansion of mercy were hanging onto that will with every ounce of strength they could muster.

All precautions were taken to secure the survival of the mission and protect its residents. No one was allowed to venture off the property except by permission. When radio and television reports suggested that random checkpoints were going on in the area, no one on Carson Hill walked outside the mansion for even a stroll around the property, not until the checkpoints were removed. The temporary quarantine was burdensome, but an all-important essential rule. The van was kept hidden in the garage. Rachael informed the BBO that no victims would be picked up or allowed to travel to the mansion until checkpoints were stopped.

Immediately following a ten-day government checkpoint in the metropolitan area of Detroit, the BBO contacted Rachael once again, informing her that they were safely holding a single thirty-two-year-old mother named Connie Powell, and her five-year-old son, Nathan. Stripped of all they had and left homeless, they needed the comfort and protection of the mission. Connie previously worked as a secretary on the surgical floor at the McDougal Hospital in Howell. Like Paul and Karen Hopkins, she had refused to be counted by the new world organization and declined to have her paycheck deposited into the system. She knew the consequences of making such a decision, even if it meant putting her son Nathan at risk of being taken away from her. An explanation for her actions could only be found in one simple reality, her faith in the Holy Scriptures. Yet that faith was severely challenged each time she looked at Nathan and realized that they might be separated before she found refuge. She could never bear being parted from him, yet obedience to the commands of the Holy Scriptures and the inner Voice that spoke so clearly to her spirit was convincing. *"I will never leave you nor forsake you."*

Once the hospital got word that she would not conform, her employment was immediately terminated. All services to her apartment were shut off. She and her son were in great immediate need.

To her advantage, before leaving the hospital, Connie overheard talk from a fellow worker about the underground network of the BBO. She refrained from questioning the worker, sensing that his attitude was in full support of Chimera and extremely negative toward the BBO. The bit of information she got suggested that help could be found in churches. She set out on foot in search of aid, hoping to find a church that secretly operated with the underground.

Time was critical. The authorities would be looking for her as soon as the information from the hospital reached their computers. A government staff worker would receive the assignment to apprehend her. She would be put in jail, maybe even killed, and Nathan would become a ward of the state. Her rescue by the BBO needed to be immediate.

Many others like Connie would be helplessly left behind because there were not enough underground networks and hidden places of mercy to help the hundreds of defecting citizens. There was no sense of fairness in anything, even within the Christian realm. Many wealthy conservatives were managing to stay free of The Great Ten Nations' system by using their possessions to barter for the things they needed. But in time, they would also come to ruin.

Connie miraculously found the BBO through a network of churches working together. She and her son Nathan were taken into safety at a Community Church, where she would be held until Rachael could transport her to the mansion.

Chimera had created a deluge of fear in those who refused to comply, but it was also creating a huge measure of confusion and anger in those who had surrendered. *Are we better off* was the question people were asking. Their pockets felt emptier, and their pursuit of happiness was quenched. Their incentive for excelling and getting ahead was gone. The backlash was obvious. The world government had reduced the masses to mortal robots, and the truth of its deceits was beginning to incite rebellion in the streets. Bouts of anarchy broke out in every major city throughout the world. Killing for no apparent reason was a daily happening. Towns and communities, once orderly and safe from crime, were in turmoil. Robbery, rape, and felonies of all sorts were rampant. The effects of Chimera spawned anarchy. The masses were on a free-for-all, intoxicated by the same mysterious force that created Chimera. Evil was spawning evil. Where once there was cheering, there was now oppression. Where once there was merry-making and music was played in the street and beautiful opera was sung in the theaters, there was now despair. Celebrations ceased, investments plummeted, Stock Markets crashed, and prices sky rocked.

Archer Holton, the mastermind of the chaos, along with the leaders of The Great Ten Nations, were recalculating their ideology and questioning the saneness of their brainchild, but they were still determined that it could work. Their scheme was created to be embraced with pleasure and great exhilaration. Archer laughed and said people would throw parties and dance in the streets. Yet in third world countries the masses were rioting because they were confused. Many of the poor were hoarding what little they had for fear they would die of hunger. Military forces frantically worked to hold chaos at bay, while the new system continued full steam ahead across the globe. The Ten Great Nations would make their scheme work even if they had to wipe out one-third of the population.

Rachael was well aware of what was coming. Soon there would arise a ruler of great importance with charismatic power, who would bring peace through false pretense. He would charm the masses with his great orations. His magnetic personality and good looks would captivate the world, and he would claim to have the power to turn chaos into order and seemingly bring the world out of the hell hole it had slipped into. He would act like God, but his intent would be to gain the entire world, taking it away from The Great Ten Nations and putting it into the palm of his hand.

People were ripe for this type of leader, but the stage was not fully set. God was in control while the clock was ticking. Though the hour had not yet arrived, the vineyards were ripe, and the wine-press of evil was full, like a malignant sore ready to burst. Whether knowingly or not, the world was at a climax, awaiting the arrival of its deliverer. Good or evil? Which would it be? In the meantime, no place was safe for those who were insubordinate to Chimera, except to hide in the secret areas known only to the BBO. Those were the places under protection of the shadow of The Almighty.

******

Shortly after Connie and her son had arrived, the Martin Montgomery family of five, from Trenton, Michigan, were brought to the mansion. Taking into consideration the beds they required, Rachael insisted that they occupy the master suite. Like all the others, this Christian family lost everything, surviving with only the clothes on their backs. Without warning, government agents suddenly evicted them at gunpoint from their home. Martin, an engineer at Ford Motor Company, and his wife, Laura, wandered the streets with their ten-year-old twin sons, Connor and Charles, and their thirteen-year-old daughter, Susan. The government's actions, though far from kind, were actually a miracle. They had somehow escaped incarceration and were able to stay together as a family. Martin determined that even if they had to stay on the streets for a short time, he would find a rescue mission somewhere.

Hours after their eviction, with darkness moving in like cumu-lous clouds without rain, they assumed it was safe to walk the streets and search for help. They had no other recourse but to keep walking and hunting. With the children whining and Laura's feet hurting because she was torn from the house without shoes, they stumbled upon a tiny church situated in the middle of a long block of small framed houses. A dim light glowed behind the basement windows that were made of thick glass blocks for privacy. Unbeknownst to Martin, the men of the church were engrossed in a secret meeting, exchanging information and planning their own escapes. It seemed to him that someone was in the basement of the church; otherwise there would be no light behind the glass block window.

He knew no one would hear a knock on the front doors of the church, so he took a small stone and tapped on the block window. Noticing a door at the rear of the church, he motioned for Laura and the children to wait there. Again he tapped on the window. Finally, someone cracked the back door open just enough to see Laura and the children standing in the darkness. Immediately the kind man threw the door wide open and ushered Laura and the children into the church, with Martin following swiftly behind.

"Oh, God bless you," Laura cried, as she helped the children into the church and down the steps to the basement.

The man guiding them had a neatly trimmed beard and appeared to be of retirement age. He kept motioning for them to follow him down the stairs and into the boiler room where there were eight men sitting on folding chairs.

"We've lost everything today," Martin said. "The authorities charged into our house with guns and forced us onto the streets."

"That kind of thing is happening all over," the bearded man said. "When the authorities get word that someone is trying to avoid

Chimera, they waste no time getting to them. You're lucky they did not take you to jail and separate you."

Thankful that they had found a safe haven, Martin and his family slept on church pews, waiting for dawn and the hope of finding a place to stay. The church men informed the nearest BBO that they had five homeless people.

In less than twenty-four hours and beyond all expectations, Martin and his family were transported safely to Carson Hill.

There was no doubt in anyone's mind at the mansion that the mission was precisely driven by Divine hands. The Spirit that was at work in the hearts of Rachael and Maggie was not simply a plan to survive, but a demonstration of God's perfect wisdom and love.

Although it was tragic that Martin and his family lost their home and all their assets, the mission needed another man to help with the heavy work. God's perfect plan was further orchestrated by Laura Montgomery's teaching degree. She would join Rose in organizing and implementing schooling for the children.

******

The mission was running like a well-oiled machine. Everyone had responsibilities and duties. Connie helped Lillian in the kitchen and in between meals worked with Maggie to keep the laundry done. Although each family was assigned a specific laundry day, towels and sheets were Maggie's responsibility, along with other domestic chores she tended to each day. Each resident was in charge of keeping their room tidy and pitching in when an extra hand was needed. Children had specific hours for study and play. The operation was much like a commune.

******

Rachael started her day as usual, walking through the mansion like a supervisor in a warehouse, checking to make sure everything was good. Today, however, her sense of confidence was interrupted when she was informed that Stacey Hopkins wasn't feeling well. The little girl slept throughout the night but woke with a 102-degree fever.

Rachael became extremely worried, not simply about Stacey, but alarmed about the probability of sickness invading the mansion.

"This is very serious, not just for Stacey but for all of us," she said to Karen. "I will try to get Dr. Kendall here as soon as possible."

She left the child's bedside and immediately went into the library to find Dr. Kendall's phone number. Rummaging through the papers on her desk, she found his business card, among useless documents of unimportant matters that had been deliberately placed in plain sight to distract any government agent who might enter the mansion on a search.

"Dr. Kendall, this is Rachael Garrison," she said when he picked up her call.

"Oh, I was planning to call you this evening. How are you?" he shot back enthusiastically.

"I'm fine, but I have an eight-year-old girl who is running a high fever. I'm wondering what I should do?"

Both Rachael and Kendall knew that they should not give more information than necessary during the call. The government was tapping phones and listening to chatter randomly. Kendall briefly informed her to start the child on an antibiotic and give her one children's strength Tylenol every four hours, along with plenty of fluids.

"Keep tabs on her fever," he said, "and if it goes to 103, sponge her down with cool water. Keep her quarantined in her room, and I'll be out to check on her tomorrow."

"Wonderful," Rachael replied. "I'll see you then."

"Yes," Kendall answered, "and by the way, the reason I was planning to call you was to tell you I would be bringing two guests with me tomorrow."

Guest was the buzz word for victim. With that, he cut the conversation off quickly and hung up, not giving any further information.

There was only one bedroom left. When it was filled, families would have to double up, or she would have to turn the game room into a bedroom, rather than the clinic area. But that would be tomorrow's concern. Today her concern was for Stacey.

THROUGHOUT THE DAY, RACHAEL CHECKED with Karen to see how the child was doing. The Tylenol helped to keep the fever down, but the little girl seemed very ill. Maggie was summoned to her bedside to join Rachael.

"I am very worried about this child, and I want us to pray for her," Rachael confided to Maggie.

"I think this is needed; she looks extremely ill," Maggie said, frowning with concern. Then looking at Karen, she motioned for her to join them.

Praying together was something Maggie and Rachael frequently did, whether there were surmounting difficulties or not. It was a natural spiritual thing, and often Maggie would sing when God's presence filled the atmosphere.

The three women stood close to the bed, looking down upon the little girl. Her cheeks were pink with fever, and her heartbeat could be seen in her neck, showing the strong pulses pushing hard in an effort to send healing blood cells throughout her body. Sick little eyes steadied on them, as though there was healing in their presence. Rachael gently laid her hand on the little girl's warm forehead and prayed the first prayer. Then Maggie prayed another prayer, so free and pure, so right to the point. Stacey needed healing, and God was able to do it.

At Maggie's concluding amen, Karen started to cry, as though she knew the situation was serious and her little girl was in danger.

"Oh now, Miss Karen, don't cry," Maggie said, gathering her into her arms and giving her a big hug. "She's going to be okay. God will see to that."

Stacey coughed and then faintly asked for a drink of water.

"I'll get it for her," Karen said. "You both go about what you were doing. I'll call you if there's any change."

Reluctantly, Rachael took the offer to get some things done before Dr. Kendall arrived the next day, and Maggie went back into the laundry room, shoving sheets and towels into the washers. She was softly humming an old hymn, as though she knew the little girl would be all right.

MORNING ARRIVED WITH BRIGHT SUNSHINE, although the Irish Hills were covered with an arctic cold mass, making its way south from Canada. At the stroke of eight, Lillian and Connie had breakfast ready to serve. Rachael knocked at the Hopkins' quarters and leaned in to check on Stacey. It was late last night when she got the last report, and at that time Stacey's temperature was still high. But to her amazement, the child was sitting up in bed, watching television.

"Well, good morning," she said with a pleased and relieved tone. "You look much better, Stacey."

"Ah huh," Stacey said, while keeping her eyes glued to the kid's program she was watching.

"It was about three a.m. when her fever broke, and she began to look and feel much better," Karen said in a voice that rang with joy.

Rachael glanced around the room, noticing how everything was in good order. The door to the walk-in closet was open, and she could see that the clothes the BBO had given them were neatly hung on hangers and shoes were placed in a straight line against the closet wall. This family was following the rules of the mission to the letter. But even if a family were messy, she wasn't sure if she had the grit to say something to them. Every family was different, and Rachael was fast learning how challenging diversity can be.

Glancing back at Karen, she said, "That's wonderful that the fever broke. Dr. Kendall will check her over when he comes today. I'll have Connie bring some breakfast up to both of you."

She gave Karen a quick hug and went downstairs to join the others in the dining room, observing that her hungry residents were graciously seated and waiting for her. With grace delivered, she glanced across the table, noticing that Stacey's brother, Michael, was all spruced up. His hair was slicked with mousse, and he was wearing a colorful sweatshirt. "You look mighty handsome this morning, Michael," she said.

He blushed, answering, "Yes ma'am," and picked up a spoon to begin eating his cereal. His father reached around him and patted his back as if he, too, were complimenting the boy. The sight of everyone neatly dressed and eagerly eating breakfast was reassuring. Yet there was a rush of doubt in Rachael's mind. She could not help wondering if anyone else would get sick.

While everyone enjoyed cold cereal, sweet canned peaches, and powdered milk that had been mixed with water the night before and refrigerated to make it more palatable, Rachael informed them that two new residents would be arriving with Dr. Kendall today.

"I don't know who these new people are, but we have one bedroom open, so I will assign rooms accordingly if I need to make changes."

No one seemed worried about space problems, so Rachael abandoned her concerns for the time being. Morning chores came immediately after breakfast, and everyone hurried off in different directions. Rachael put on a heavy sweater and went outside to check the premises and then gave in to her urge to walk into the abandoned stables.

Pushing the heavy door open, she breathed in deeply. The smell of hay faintly remained, reminding her of the beautiful quarter horses she once owned. She put her hand to her mouth, as though to stifle the need to cry. *Oh, Grant, I miss you and the horses and our life as we knew it*, she said to herself, realizing that everything she loved was gone, everything but the mansion.

She returned to the library to make notes in her log and study the inventory sheets that noted the remaining supplies and food. The inventory log was kept hidden in the wall safe behind a picture in the library. Each family helped keep track of everything they used by turning in slips that noted if something was empty or getting low, or a new bottle or package was opened. A separate log was kept by Lillian of the food supply. So far, there were no shortages. The gargantuan buying that Maggie and Lillian accomplished before Chimera became law was sufficient for the time being. It would be a few weeks before bartering would be necessary.

She put the log and the inventory sheets under the wool oriental area rug in front of the leather couch, not wanting to lock it back into the wall safe. She could retrieve it quickly when Kendall arrived. She wanted him to see how well they were doing, and surely, he would want to give a report to the BBO back in Troy.

There was something about him coming today that was stirring excitement in her. She blushed to think about it. Dare she entertain these feelings that were surfacing? Could she admit that she felt excited?

Lillian and Connie began preparing the lunch menu with the expectation that Kendall and the two new residents would come in time for the meal. Connie rolled out biscuit dough while Lillian prepared a vegetable chicken stew by selecting canned chicken, frozen peas and carrots, canned shortcut green beans, and cream of chicken soup for the gravy. Juice replaced the green salad missing from their diets. Today a small glass of tomato juice would be served as a complimentary side. Aware that Dr. Kendall Saunders' visit was special, and anticipating he would stay for the evening meal, Lillian brought several cans of peaches up from the basement and made a cobbler. If he didn't stay, the treat would still be savored.

While she and Connie worked in the kitchen, Nathan and Michael played upstairs in the master suite with Connor and Charles. Their laughter and voices were as wonderful as a symphony orchestra resonating throughout the mansion. Amid all the anxieties and the afflictions of so many destitute people in the world, the children were like sunbeams that colored the darkness.

Susan seemed like the fifth wheel around the mansion, mostly because she was the oldest child and missed the company of her friends. But she took a shine to Maggie, and it made everyone feel better. Maggie had that special gift that drew anyone stuck in the dumps to her for counsel and just *plain old love.* Susan took to her like a puppy takes to a little boy. Almost every day, after her homework was completed, she tailed Maggie around the house, helping her with the domestic chores and listening to Maggie's interesting talk. The teenager had never befriended a black person before, so Maggie was a unique and special personality that the young girl was drawn to.

IT WAS ALMOST NOON WHEN Kendall drove up the circular driveway of the mansion with the new residents. Rachael heard Duke bark, signaling that someone was approaching. She glanced out the grand room windows to see the van moving slowly up the driveway. She opened the doors and stepped out on the porch, shivering in the cold wind that circled the gothic pillars.

Kendall quickly opened the van door and motioned for Rachael to come and take his medical bag, which he held up for her to see. He then stepped to the side of the van and opened the sliding door. An elderly lady, dressed in dark slacks and a heavy wool coat was sitting in the seat near the door. She grabbed hold of Kendall's hand and stepped out of the van, her dark eyes wide with amazement as she looked at the mansion. The wind ruffled her black gray-streaked hair. She turned and waited for Kendall to help her elderly husband. The old man strained as he leaned forward to take the doctor's hand and worked hard to inch himself up toward the edge of the seat. Slowly, as though his bones were too stiff and sluggish to move, he hobbled out of the van.

His hair was completely white, framing a face wrinkled with years. He wore dark brown slacks and a pair of Nike running shoes that seemed a bit odd for an old man. A short winter jacket, plumped with polyester fluff, was worn over a checkered flannel shirt. The bulk made him look twice as large as he really was.

Shivering and standing with Kendall's medical bag in her hand, Rachael said a quick hello and waited for the couple to follow her into the mansion. But instead of following her, the couple stood looking into the van, while Kendall climbed inside. Rachael squinted in the sunlight and saw him emerge from the van, carefully holding a bundle wrapped in a blanket that he eased into the old lady's arms. Rachael's heart leaped as she saw a tiny baby with snow-white skin and jet-black hair nestled in the blanket.

"Oh my goodness," she squealed with interest. "Let's get this baby inside where it's warm."

Kendall went back into the van and brought out a car seat and a diaper bag, while Rachael led the couple to the doors of the mansion. Once inside, she extended her hand to the old man.

"I'm Rachael Garrison, director of the Carson Hill Mission and owner of the mansion," she said to the couple. She shook the old man's hand.

"Glad to meet you," the old man said. "I'm Peter Rubinstein, and this is my wife, Esther."

"So happy to meet you," she replied while glancing at them and then looking at the baby bunched in Esther's arms. She set the medical bag down and reached her hands out.

"Here, let me take the baby."

Kendall entered the door and set the car seat and the diaper bag into the entrance hall while muttering something about having a bassinet in the back of the van and several packages of diapers. He turned and went back to the van.

He had not come empty-handed. He brought two crates of canned formula, several baby bottles, and baby clothes. The van was full of baby things that the BBO had managed to deliver to him the night before. Through some miracle of underground networking, they had come up with the basic supplies for this baby.

Now that everyone was inside, Kendall began telling Rachael about the baby.

"Shortly after I talked with you on the phone yesterday, the BBO called and said they had an abandoned baby that had been dropped off at a church where one of the underground pastors is employed. We discussed briefly where the baby should be taken.

"Turning it over to the authorities would be risky and might put the whole operation at risk. So, we decided the child should be brought here, where you have a safe place and the facilities to care for it."

While Kendall was explaining all this, Rachael was unwrapping the baby, which suddenly decided to cry.

"There, there," Rachael said softly as she cuddled the baby close.

"Is this a girl or boy," she asked, not wanting to peek into the diaper and check out the anatomy.

"It's a baby girl," Esther said sharply.

Rachael was a little taken aback by Esther's sharp tone.

"Now Esther, calm down," Peter said to her. "This child is in good hands, and you know that Dr. Luke's son is capable of telling Mrs. Garrison how to take care of it."

By now, the whole household was in the entrance hall gaping at the baby. Maggie took the child out of Rachael's arms, grabbed up the diaper bag, and said, "I think she needs a diaper change after that long ride." With that, she took the baby into the library.

Introductions were made for those who were yet to meet Dr. Kendall Saunders officially. Esther and Peter were introduced to the other residents, and Connie took their coats.

In all of this commotion, silent gratefulness swept over Rachael. She had plenty of room for these guests. The new residents were married and would occupy the last bedroom. No bunching up would be required. As for the baby, she was already entertaining ideas.

THE BISCUITS WERE BAKING, AND the chicken stew was heating, while everyone talked with the new Rubinstein couple and ogled over the baby. Lillian interrupted with the announcement that lunch would be served in just a few minutes. While all this commotion was going on, Kendall was anxious to see the sick child, so taking his medical bag in hand, he asked Rachael to direct him to her.

"She's much better today," Rachael told him while they climbed the staircase. "Her fever broke early this morning."

Stacey was up and dressed in a pair of soft pink sweat pants with matching top, coloring in her favorite book when Kendall and Rachael walked into the bedroom. Quick introductions were made to Karen, and without further words, he opened his bag, pulled out a stethoscope, an ear light, a tongue depressor, and a thermometer and began his examination.

"I think she probably had a virus that was short-lived," he said. "It's common for kids to recover things quickly. If she had a bacterial infection, she would still be running a temperature and feeling sick."

Rachael noticed how handsome he looked as he examined the young girl and talked softly to her. She felt a silly flutter, which took her by surprise and almost made her blush. *Oh please, let's not entertain this,* she said to herself. Quickly regaining her senses, she put every thought in her imagination into strict solitary confinement.

"Are you hungry, Stacey?" Kendall asked her.

"Yes," shaking her head up and down.

"I think I can say it's safe for you to join the others for lunch," and with that, he closed his medical bag and was ready to leave the room.

"I hope you'll stay and eat with us, Dr. Saunders," Rachael inquired, calling him by his professional name in front of the others. "In fact, I am hoping you can stay long enough to view my log and inventory sheets to see how well the mission is running. I'm sure the BBO would like a report. Maybe even stay for dinner this evening."

"Yes, I'd like very much to stay."

During lunch, while the entire group sat at the long dining table enjoying the chicken stew, Rachael couldn't help but notice that Kendall often looked her way, as though to study her in an admiring way. She almost blushed at his glances. *What's happening here,* she asked herself.

The baby was now sleeping in the bassinet near her place at the head of the table. It seemed right to keep the motherless child close. She took the baby up into her arms.

There was something wonderful about this afternoon. The simple chicken stew filled empty stomachs, and the happy chatter around the table filled lonesome hearts. Kendall answered questions about the underground and how it was fairing around the country. He, in turn, asked questions of them. A sense of family filled the mansion. For the first time in weeks, Rachael felt secure and comfortable.

Most every day, she felt the strain of responsibility, but today was different. Was it the baby that was making the difference? Was it Kendall's presence? She wasn't sure. But what she did know was that the entire excitement of this day, meeting new people, being asked to take care of a tiny motherless baby, and Dr. Kendall Saunders sitting at her table brought joy.

Rachael then asked Laura and Karen to take the baby's things to her bedroom.

"The baby will stay with me," she said.

Everyone's eyes opened wide, and heads turned to her direction. Some were thinking that Karen or Laura would keep the baby; being mothers, they seemed more appropriate.

Paul offered to take the bassinet up and stack the extra diapers in the medical closet. Rachael was already thinking far ahead. She would make a nursery for the baby in her bedroom, and if the BBO found no claim to the child, she would keep the little one as her own.

Everyone scattered to different places while Kendall and Rachael went to the library to discuss the mission's progress. She pulled the log sheets out from underneath the rug, smiling while Kendall laughed at her creative caution.

"I try to cover all my bases and not make any mistakes," she said, referring to her creative hiding place under the rug.

They sat on the leather couch with the inventory sheets and the log spread out on the long bunching table in front of them. Kendall studied the paperwork while hearing from her the explanations of how well the mission was going. She explained every detail and the importance of following the Mission Plan to the letter so that the authorities would not discover their hideaway. She knew he was listening carefully, but what she didn't know was that he was not only interested in her mission but also impressed with her sophistication and beauty.

Listening to her talk, he wanted to know everything about her, what her parents were like, where she was schooled, how she managed to be so successful in real estate, why she lived in the Irish Hills of Michigan rather than a palace on the ocean or a rambling estate in a big city. She fascinated him, and letting his feelings go un-chased, he found himself wanting to hug her.

Rachael enjoyed their conversation while at the same time felt uncomfortable because Grant had been dead less than a year and another man was sharing interest in the Plan that he helped organize. He should be the one talking with this doctor, not lying in a grave. Even with those guarded thoughts, Kendall's presence was making her aware of the emptiness she was suffering. The sound of his voice, the way he looked at her, the way he touched her arm on occasion, made her come alive in a new way. She couldn't help but feel her loneliness.

The time to leave came much too soon, but before going, Kendall addressed the baby's needs, especially the need for round-the-clock scheduled feedings. He told Rachael how to make a sufficient formula out of what she had in the pantry, should the formula he brought run out.

"Hopefully, the BBO can get more, but if not, this recipe will keep the baby healthy until we can start her on strained foods," he said. The recipe consisted of measured amounts of powdered milk, boiled water, and a little light Karo Syrup.

"In a couple of weeks, she should be started on baby cereal," he continued. "I will try to get everything you need from the BBO and make another trip in about ten days."

Then, looking seriously at her, he said, "You call me if there are any problems."

"I will, and thank you for all you have done," she answered, feeling her heart leap at the mention that he would be back in a few days.

After a farewell to everyone, he stopped on the porch and looked back. Rachael stepped forward and walked with him to the van.

"You're a wonderful person," he said to her, as they stood on the circle drive. He reached for her hand and drew it up to his mouth and lightly kissed it. He could be giving a signal that he was interested in her as a woman, as well as someone running a rescue mission. Or, his gesture could be a polite way of showing respect and appreciation for her. He said nothing more, but climbed into the van and started the engine.

"Be careful on your way back," she told him. "Give my regards to your father and tell those working with the underground how much I appreciate them."

"I will," he said.

She watched the van until it was out of sight. Her heart reeling in a thousand pleasant directions, and with its spinning there were just as many emotions dancing on strings. Whatever he meant by kissing her hand, she could only guess. Unaware of the chilling air and her shivering, she walked slowly back inside, lifting the hand Kendall kissed to her mouth and gently brushing it across her lips. Was she falling in love? She dared not answer.

THE EXPERIENCE OF HAVING A baby in her room delighted her. She and Grant wanted a baby, but it never happened. Now, this tiny infant, whose mother had abandoned it for reasons no one knew, was filling Rachael's heart with something new and wonderful.

She looked at her, sleeping so peacefully in the bassinet. Tears filled her eyes as she thought of the child's mother, possibly loving the baby, but abandoning it because she had no other choice. She bowed her head and thanked God for the tiny human life that had come to the mansion.

"I shall name her Mary Elizabeth, and I will call her Beth," she said in a soft voice. Then leaned down and kissed the tiny forehead, hoping that no one would seek after the child.

It was late when she undressed and slipped into the shower, letting the water pour over her body like warm rain on a summer's day. *If only the cares of this world could be washed away, as easy as taking a shower,* she thought. She dried quickly and put on silk pajamas. Then, looking toward Beth, who was sleeping soundly, she dimmed the overhead light and turned on the Tiffany floor lamp near her desk. Sitting down in the satin covered boudoir chair, she reached for a pen and wrote in her journal:

> *November 12. In the midst of darkness and despair, in a world that follows after false precepts and is bound under the rule of tyranny, the God of all Gods has comforted me with the presence of a tiny baby and a doctor named Kendall. How is it that I should be so blessed? I know not the answer. But this one thing I rejoice in, the certainty that I can take refuge in God, just as this baby takes refuge in me. God will scatter my enemies and keep this child safe. He will bring justice for Grant's death. He will bring down the mighty from their high seats. He will not turn His back on those who honor Him. In my mansion of plenty, God has filled my hungry heart.*

CHAPTER 5

FALLING IN LOVE WITH LOVE ONCE MORE

FAMILIARITY SOMETIMES BREEDS CONTEMPT, AND in the case of Esther Rubinstein that was no understatement. She was a strong, opinionated Jewish woman, who had converted to Christianity in her senior years. Coming to know her was like brushing up against a barberry bush. Like most converts, she was enthusiastic about her newly found faith and ready to debate anyone who dared differ from her religious philosophy.

It was after a peaceful dinner that things started to get a little controversial. The brocade drapes were pulled, and everyone had settled into their favorite places in the grand room to relax before going to bed. Esther and Peter were sitting comfortably on the oversized love seat, while the others were settled on the long sectional and into other comfortable chairs. Everyone was watching a television program featuring biographies of historical people, their famous marks in history, and their burials. For some unknown reason, the program spurred the subject of cremation.

"Funeral costs have sky-rocketed so high that a lot of people are opting to be cremated rather than pay for embalming and visitation,"

Martin innocently commented, not knowing why he was actually saying this.

"That's for sure," Karen joined in. "In fact, most of my relatives have been cremated. It's becoming a popular choice."

Esther's eyebrows went up. If there was one subject that she took offense to, it was the subject of cremation.

"I don't think it's Christian," she snorted. "I mean, why would a person want to burn the body God created, even if it is dead?"

Everyone stared at her, instantly feeling forewarned to pass up the debate that Esther was obviously initiating.

She continued, "It's disrespectful. Just look at Jesus. No one burned his body. On the contrary, Mary Magdalene came to the tomb to anoint His body after he died."

Peter patted her leg as if to say calm down and be quiet, but it didn't silence her.

"When I think of burning human flesh, I think of hell. I think of Auschwitz. Cremation is evil. My brother and his whole family were burned to ashes at Auschwitz. First, they gassed them, then they burned them up in hot ovens and shoveled their ashes in wheelbarrows and paved roads with them."

Her voice got louder. "Such disrespect for the human body!"

She paused for a moment, while every eye was on her, and every ear in the grand room was listening with new respect.

"Disgusting and evil . . . that's what cremation is," she continued. "I do not want my body burned when I die. I will be buried like Christ."

There was no doubt that these rescued residents were a widely diverse group of individuals. All of them embraced Christianity, but each family and each individual brought with them their own convictions and religious doctrine.

Rachael wasn't sure if she should stop Esther from saying anything more. So far, there prevailed a common oneness within the circle, and no referee was needed. When it came to Esther, however, few challenged her opinions, and if they did, it was always done with respect. Tonight, no one challenged her, so Rachael was content to relax, thinking everyone's silence was in agreement to let the precious woman talk.

******

Baby Beth was showing signs of recognizing Rachael's voice. Although the days were busy with mission work, Rachael deliberately found time to feed and hold Beth and talk to her. The baby woke every morning and went to sleep every night to the sound of her voice. She knew her touch. She knew her loving arms. Maggie and the others were spoiling her whenever possible. She was one blessed little baby. Yet somewhere in the city of Detroit, Beth's mother might still be living and longing for her baby. Rachael often thought, *why was this child found on the doorsteps of a church? Could she be ordained of God for a purpose no one yet knows? What could be the providence behind this?*

Susan made an ideal built-in babysitter, but Maggie and the others were always opting for their time to hold and love this little one. Only when she slept was Beth without attention. The BBO had no word about the infant's mother, so Rachael was pulling the child into her life as her very own, even referring to herself as "Mama." There was a sense of jubilation in the mansion, brought about because of the joy a baby generates. Still, Kendall occupied many of Rachael's thoughts. She desired to call him but didn't want to appear bold and anxious. What would she use as her excuse to telephone him? After all, things were running smoothly, and the baby was taking her formula well. He had promised to return in a few days. Best to wait for his call.

SHE DROPPED THE THOUGHT OF calling Kendall and propped herself up in the bed, reading while Beth slept in the bassinet next to her. Suddenly the phone rang, piercing the silence.

"Rachael, this is Kendall, how's everything going?"

Her heart began to pound as though it would leap from her chest. The sound of Dr. Kendall Saunders' voice thrilled her as if she were a high school girl with a crush for the first time.

"Everything is fine, Kendall," she said, trying not to appear overly excited. "Is everything all right at your end?"

"Everything is good. I'm wondering how the baby is doing and also if Stacey is still feeling well."

"Oh, they're both fine," she replied. "I've named the baby Mary Elizabeth, and we are calling her Beth."

"Mary Elizabeth," he said softly as though it were a melody. "I like that name, Mary Elizabeth, it sounds so supreme, like a princess of royal blood." He chuckled.

There was an awkward silence for a moment. Rachael wasn't sure what she should say next.

"I just wanted to call and see if everything is going well," he said, breaking the silence. "I miss everyone on Carson Hill."

"We miss you, too," she confessed to him. "I . . . I was going to call you, but I didn't think I should. I know you're very busy."

"Well, I'm coming out tomorrow if that's okay," he continued. "I know I said I'd be back in ten days, but the BBO has given me more formula and diapers and cereal for the baby. I've been able to find a used baby crib as well, so I want to bring everything tomorrow if I won't upset your schedule."

"Upset my schedule," Rachael laughed. "Not at all, I'm happy to have you here anytime." If she was honest, she would tell him how she was counting the days for his return.

He chuckled again.

"My father is taking my patients for the next two days, so if you can put me up in the game room, I'll stay and do some physical exams on the older folks. I probably should monitor their medications too. You know, just make sure they are doing okay."

He was referring to Peter and Esther, and Rose, who were on diuretics for heart problems.

"That's great," Rachael confirmed. "We'll get the game room ready for you. Paul and Martin can move the extra bed that is in Rose's room. What time do you think you'll be here?"

If Rachael knew his thoughts after asking that question, she would know he wanted to come as soon as possible, and she would know that he wanted very much to be with her.

"I'm planning to leave here about seven tomorrow morning, so I should be there by nine. My van is already packed. I disassembled the crib just a while ago and have it loaded. So, I'll see you in the morning."

"We'll all be waiting. Drive carefully."

Without any further talk, he bid her goodnight. She turned her phone off and laid back against the pillows, feeling as though she were moving through a beautiful dream. She pictured herself as a princess, donning a beautiful gown, and Kendall as a knight in shining armor. *So corny,* she thought, but indeed he seemed valiant in every respect. He had come to help her, to protect her, perhaps to love her. She couldn't explain how her attraction to him had happened so suddenly, and why she was embracing it without many reservations. She didn't want to explain it. She simply was allowing it to happen.

Too excited to sleep, she put her robe on and went down to the kitchen. She noticed that the other bedroom doors were closed as she passed by them. The mansion was quiet. Everyone was sleeping. Lillian, however, was still in the kitchen, checking her menu for tomorrow and bringing her food log up to date.

"Well, Miss Rachael, you're up and about rather late," she said, as she hung the clipboard on a nail in the pantry.

"I couldn't sleep," Rachael answered. "Kendall called. He's coming tomorrow and will be spending a couple of days here."

"Great!" Lillian commented, catching the happiness in Rachael's eyes and smiled.

"You're falling for that handsome doctor," she said with a tease.

"Does it show?" she asked.

"It shows, and I think it's wonderful. You don't need to be without a man, running a mission like this in a crazy world. You need a partner like him at your side."

Rachael despised the word *partner.* It held a certain unchristian, unspiritual connotation. The world was full of *partners,* and many of these relationships were invalid and sinful according to God's precepts and principles. But with Lillian's approval (not that she needed her approval), she was relieved and assumed that Maggie would also feel the same way. Still, she worried about how it looked with regard to Grant.

"I don't want to be disrespectful to Grant's memory," she went on. "He was my husband for many years, and I loved him more than anyone else. But he's gone, and Kendall is here, alive and wonderful. I know he is drawn to me the same way I am drawn to him, I'm just sure of that by the way he talks to me and the way he looks at me."

She studied Lillian's face as she spoke, waiting to see how she would react to what she was revealing to her.

"Rachael, dear, you have nothing to be ashamed of." And with that said, she hugged her. "I'm sure Grant would be the first one to give his approval. If he could talk to you right now, he would say, *go for it girl*. You do what your heart is telling you to do, and don't worry about what others may think."

Rachael felt relieved, even surprised, that something so intimate had transpired between her and Lillian. Things were usually always business between them. Lillian was consistently reserved, never disclosing her feelings, but her words tonight were like a sister, wanting the best for someone they loved.

"Be sure to figure another person into the meals for the next two days," Rachael said as she turned to leave the kitchen. "He will be here sometime after breakfast."

******

The baby woke when the first signs of morning peeked through the half-closed shutters. Her soft sounds were like a musical sonnet filling the room. *Like the song of the first robin in springtime or a harp softly played under the willow.*

Maggie knocked at the door offering a warm bottle for Beth.

"Just like clockwork, she's awake and waiting for this," Rachael said, taking the bottle.

Maggie sat down in the boudoir chair, watching Rachael lift Beth from the bassinet.

"I hear that Dr. Saunders is coming today," she stated. "Lillian told me."

Rachael looked up and saw the smile on Maggie's face. Then she laughed rather bashfully and said, "Yes, and you're right, I'm falling in love with him, but don't dare say a word to him."

"I knew it, I knew it!" she bellowed, "and I can't think of a better match."

"You're not mad at me, with Grant not gone a year yet?"

"Of course not, child," Maggie said. "Time has nothing to do with it. When the right person comes along, it's right no matter how soon or how late."

Maggie's words were as good as Catherine Carson's words would have been if Rachael wanted a mother's blessing. Her father would also approve, she was sure of that.

"I love you, Maggie, you know that. Your blessing is all I need."

She hugged her and then cuddled Beth in her arms, putting the bottle to her little mouth. She felt assured by Maggie's words that she was not being disrespectful to Grant's memory. More settled about the guilty feelings now, and having Maggie's approval, she let her feelings for Kendall relax and bring whatever they might.

At breakfast she told the group that Kendall would be arriving and staying a couple of days. She turned to Susan. "Tomorrow, and the next day, if you don't mind, I will ask you to take Beth until bedtime, while I work with Dr. Saunders."

"That's fine with me, Mrs. Garrison."

LIKE A TEENAGER IN LOVE, Rachael fussed with her hair and makeup, making sure both were perfect. Maggie made certain that the library and the solarium were kept vacant so that Rachael and Kendall had somewhere to go if they wanted to be alone.

Everyone was getting involved with Kendall's visit, including Lillian, who was planning to serve dinner with the good china and silver. She thought she might be over-doing it, but as long as everyone was having fun acting like chaperones, she was taking her turn indulging in things to make his visit as perfect as possible. In all of this excitement, the evil world outside was pushed to the sidelines, allowing the joy that Rachael was hoping for to come to full bloom.

Not wanting to appear overly anxious, she let Maggie open the door and welcome Kendall.

"Hello, Maggie, and how are you today?" Kendall inquired in a rather chirp voice as he stepped inside.

"Oh, just fine, Dr. Saunders," she replied while taking his jacket and motioning him to the grand room.

The sound of his voice stirred Rachael's heart, igniting all sorts of emotions as she walked toward the entrance hall to greet him. It seemed to her that his eyes were dancing when he looked at her. Wild horses could not hold back their embrace. She hugged him, and they burst into laughter as if to hide their romantic feelings.

Maggie was smiling and shaking her head. Rachael knew what she was thinking—that courtships in the twenty-first century moved much faster, compared to her younger days.

For the rest of the morning, they talked and enjoyed being together, first sipping coffee in the library and then going for a walk outside, hoping it was safe to stroll through the property. Kendall took her hand as they walked, and she told him about the horses and her mother's love of riding, and how her mother, Catherine, had lost her life in a terrible collision only a few miles from the hill. He listened and occasionally stopped to look at her. She told him about her father and how he brilliantly built their real estate corporation into a multi-million-dollar business. Then, she gathered the courage to talk about Grant.

He stopped walking and listened with interest while she told him of the years she and Grant had spent together. She talked of her love for him and how their marriage was wonderful. She left nothing out. She detailed his murder and talked about Archer and Holton Computer Corporation, and how the system that the government was using to gain power and wealth belonged to this madman, whom she was sure had murdered her husband. She told him that Grant was mysteriously found by Archer at a computer symposium and was asked to work a short-term contract for him, but then later realized that the software he was working on was a system of evil worldwide control being created for The Ten Great Nations.

"He tried to stop it, you know!" Her voice sounded sorrowful, and she was almost crying.

She told him how she and Maggie found him slumped over the steering wheel in the garage of their Dearborn condo.

"He died a hero, trying to stop all this madness," she whispered, with tears in her eyes.

With all that she was telling him, Kendall's heart felt as though it would burst for her. He wanted to take her into his arms and hold her forever. Hearing the details of her life made him love her all the more. He pulled her close and stroked her hair as she leaned against him, feeling helpless to stop his affection. He kissed the tears that streamed down her cheeks and searched her eyes. Their faces moved closer. The kiss was tender, and he ended it only to kiss her again.

The two days he spent at the mansion were days of joy for everyone. He had not only gained the heart of Rachael, but was also loved and admired by everyone. He took time for each individual that came to him. Whether it was for a medical concern or a question about his medical practice in Farmington Hills, he was happy to talk, and he also asked them questions.

During both evenings of his visit, the household sat in the grand room after dinner like they always did, taking turns talking about their lives and their dreams, even for the future that was unsure. Kendall and Rachael sat close together on the couch, with Beth bundled in a blanket near them. The children seemed amused about their lovie-dovie behavior—Stacey and Susan, especially. They could not keep themselves from staring at Kendall and occasionally giggling. He noticed their bashful curiosity and was charmingly amused. He would be returning home in the morning, but his heart would be staying here, where he knew without any doubt he belonged.

At nine o'clock Martin interrupted conversations by turning on the cable news network. Getting the latest news each evening was their custom before everyone retired to their bedrooms. Breaking news was coming across the wires.

"Shhhh," he said as he motioned for everyone to be quiet and listen.

The newscaster looked into the camera and read the prompter:

Word is coming to us from many of our sources throughout the country that the government will begin an accelerated campaign to identify the people who have not complied with Chimera. There has been a great deal of buzz on the streets today regarding what steps the government will take to bring defiant people into custody, and what the punishment might be when they are found. One source tells us that to resist is an act of treason. Treason is punishable by death.

Rose gasped and put her hands up to her mouth in horror. The news continued . . .

It appears that many so-called evangelical Christians have refused the world-wide system of Chimera and are living in defiance of it. They have established underground networks to help each other. Hundreds throughout the country are involved in these networks. In a news conference this afternoon, the President said it is only a matter of time before these people will be caught and taken into custody and punished.

Everyone started talking at once.

"Let's calm down folks, and not jump to any conclusions until we know more about this," Paul said.

"He's right," Kendall interrupted. "We don't know if just one or two areas that have been found out, or if it's widespread. I think we should continue as we have been doing, and just be extremely careful. As far as we know, only a few people know where this mission is located. So, I think we can assume that you are all safe for the time being."

The chatter died down, and one by one, families went up to their quarters to begin bedding down for the night. Kendall walked Rachael and baby Beth to their room and kissed them both goodnight.

"I'm worried, Kendall, that my mission will be found out." She put Beth into her crib.

He was standing in the doorway, watching her and noticing that she had beautifully slipped into motherhood without any reluctance or inhibitions. She walked back to him and put her arms around him as if to bid him goodnight.

"I'd feel safer if you could stay here and not go back home," she continued.

He drew her close and nestled his face in her hair.

"I know you're worried," he said softly in her ear, "but I have to get back and look after things. There are things that I must do before I consider any major changes."

"You're right," she relented. "It's just that I'll miss you and worry about you."

CHAPTER 6

DEATH INVADES CARSON HILL

IT WASN'T SO MUCH THE stockpiling of goods and the interconnections of the underground networks that angered the officials running the new economic system, but rather it was the Christian's refusal to acknowledge and accept the system because of religious beliefs. This furious government attitude made everyone on Carson Hill fearful. News reports indicated that two underground networks had been discovered. The closest one to Michigan was in Indianapolis, Indiana. This network had been transferring victims to safe places from as far away as Gary, Indiana and southeastward into Louisville, Kentucky. The other network was discovered clear across the nation in Anaheim, California. There was some relief at Carson Hill because of how far away these underground networks were from the BBO in Troy, but there remained a great deal of apprehension. No one could be certain their area was not under suspicion. Their guard was up, and extreme caution was being used at every turn.

Kendall decided that it was too risky to commute back and forth from his medical practice in Farmington Hills, so he opted to permanently move into the mansion. His father agreed to take as many of his patients as possible, the majority of them being long-time friends, and many of them members of the underground in Troy.

After settling everything with his medical practice and with his father, he was on his way to the Irish Hills. He stopped at a shopping center in northeast Detroit and bartered with a stranger for a cell phone, knowing that he could no longer risk using his current phone. The barter was easy. The black market of merchandise could be found most anywhere if a person had the courage to look and had the right payment. Anyone could buy just about anything. It was a brilliant move on Kendall's part to get another cell phone. Better yet, the phone he bargained for had several thousand free minutes and could only be traced if he stayed on the line for long periods of time. If the minutes were used sparingly, he could call his father and also contact the Troy underground for things they needed at the mansion. It would be risky to use it because the government randomly listened in on cell phone chatter, but the phone could only be traced back to where he was talking from. If his conversations were kept to one minute or less, the phone would be a safe way for him and Rachael to communicate. Cell signals to a tower engaged with millions of other signals, so listening in on Kendall's short conversations would be like looking for a needle in a haystack unless an ID was known. It would take the government several minutes to find where the phone was in use.

Heading west to the mansion, his van filled with medical supplies, he made his way carefully on the freeways that interlaced around Detroit, and finally onto rural M 50. Although he would miss his parents and his medical practice, being with Rachael meant more to him than anything else.

******

The game room was turned into a combination bedroom and clinic for Kendall. Every bed had someone in it now, and there would be no more victims brought to Carson Hill. Perhaps this was a selfish decision, but the more residents Rachael housed, the faster food and other items would be used up. She was busy enough, and Kendall would also be busy tending to the growing needs of the elderly residents, especially Peter Rubinstein, who appeared to be getting weaker.

Newscasts aired dreadful scenes of the government confiscating private property and making arrests. Fear continued to mount on Carson Hill, and it was extremely hard for Rachael to conceal her nagging apprehension. The feeling of uneasiness never let up. Her thoughts often took her into gruesome realities. There would be no turning back. There was nowhere to turn back to. The mansion was the only place to hide, and she realized that if she were found out, eighteen innocent people would also be found. Still, with all the fear and apprehension she struggled with, each day went on circumspectly, and the deliberate exercise of faith sustained her and everyone else. Daily group prayer bolstered their trust. God's presence would often meet them with power so strong that a hush would come over them. When His presence was strong, no one spoke.

Draperies on all windows were closed before dark. Lights were kept low, and security was armed at all times. Whenever someone left the mansion, even to take their trash behind the stables, the security system was re-armed by someone inside.

Three knocks followed by two knocks was the established countersign to enter the mansion. No one would disarm the security system and open any of the doors unless the countersign knocks were heard. Drills continued every day to gain split-second timing getting everything and everyone out of sight.

Rachael planned special hours for quiet games with the children to keep anxiety at a minimal level. Lillian served popcorn during game time, and everyone was extremely thankful that there was a good supply of it. How ingenious that popcorn was as plenteous as staples. God was in everything, including popcorn.

The elderly people read books from Rachael's library. Esther nominated herself as the volunteer librarian, keeping track of every book that went out and came back to the shelves. The order of things served well.

******

It was ten o'clock in the morning when Esther hurried down the winding staircase to fetch Kendall.

"Dr. Saunders, hurry, something has happened to Peter," she cried as she reached Kendall in the grand room where he was watching a cable news report.

Immediately he rushed up the massive staircase, with Paul and Martin following after him. Peter was unconscious when they reached him. He was lying face down on the floor.

"Let's move him onto the bed, carefully," Kendall told Paul and Martin.

Esther began to weep loudly, as she hovered over him, touching his face and his hands, as though she might be able to wake him up. But he lay lifeless. Kendall quickly retrieved his medical bag and returned, gently pushing Esther aside. He checked his eyes and loosened his shirt, listening first to his heart and then taking his blood pressure.

"I'm afraid this looks very bad," he said to her. "My professional guess is that he's had a massive stroke. The best we can do since we have no facilities to manage such serious things is to simply keep him comfortable with pain medication and see if he rallies. The next few hours will most likely tell the story."

Esther knelt beside the bed and laid her head next to Peter. Bitterly she wept, as though her life with him had suddenly been ripped into thousands of pieces of confetti falling to the ground. Her sobbing echoed throughout the mansion, bringing the others upstairs, Rachael with them. The scene was upsetting, for there could be no plan of escaping reality. Death and illness would come to Carson Hill, and no one would hold it back. From the very beginning, Rachael instinctively knew the moment the news of the Mediterranean war went across the television screen, even before Grant was murdered, that her life was entering a realm she had never experienced before. Her emotions would be new, her thoughts grossly dissimilar to anything she had ever contemplated before.

Everyone loved Peter, this wonderful Jewish man who loved his Messiah and faithfully studied the Scriptures. Rachael slipped her arm around Kendall, sensing his sorrow that he could do nothing more for the dear man. She wiped her tears with her hand and then walked over to Esther and knelt beside her.

NIGHT WAS COMING QUICKLY. ESTHER and Kendall sat at Peter's bed, watching for any sign that would indicate he was going to rally. His chest heaved up and down with labored breathing. Even with morphine, he was struggling. His life hung in the balance.

In many respects, the desire for life is relinquished when suffering is observed by a loved one looking on, and Esther was almost willingly coming to that point. Her beloved was deteriorating and falling off, wanting to wing his way heavenward. She must let him go.

Kendall cat napped off and on in a reclining chair near the bed, often awakening when someone came to the room to peek in and offer help. Finally, by midnight the mansion was quiet, and the vigil was left to him and Esther.

Nothing changed for the better. Peter's vital signs were weakening.

"Is he in pain?" Esther questioned softly.

"Well, if he were conscious, he would be in pain," Kendall said, "but his unconsciousness and lack of movement indicate that he is probably feeling no pain. But to be sure, the morphine I am giving him every three hours will keep him comfortable."

Esther nodded and sat down in a chair between the bed and the recliner. She was weary.

"Why don't you take the recliner and sleep?" Kendall offered. "I will watch Peter and wake you if there is any change."

"Oh, I don't know if I could sleep."

"Well, you try anyway," he insisted.

With that, Esther slipped into the recliner and closed her eyes, allowing her weary body to rest while she waited for her husband to wake up.

IN THE WEE HOURS OF the morning, while she slept and Kendall nodded off, Peter slipped away. Quietly, without any strain or struggle, he took his last breath.

A NEW AND AGONIZING DIMENSION invaded Carson Hill, *death*, with all its coldness and grief. Yet more than the dreadful precedent it brought to them, was the serious dilemma of what to do with Peter's body?

"We can't take him to a funeral home," Martin said. "We'll be found out for sure if we do."

"He's right," Rose said. "But maybe the BBO knows of a funeral home that would take him."

"We can't transfer a dead body all the way to Troy," Martin said rather abruptly.

Rachael stood quietly while the others talked, and when everyone had finished speaking she said, "We will bury Peter on the premises; there's no other way." Everyone remained silent for a few seconds while what she said dug in.

"Rachael is right," Paul said, breaking the silence. "We will have to dig during the night hours tonight and bury Peter while it is dark. I would suggest that we have his funeral and burial committal right here at his bedside today. We three men can dig the grave as soon as the sun goes down, but there should be no talking while we are outside. Noise and voices can travel downhill and even across the lake."

Everyone agreed, even Esther, who was no longer crying.

Kendall and Martin prepared Peter's body for burial, washing and shaving him, and putting on his best clothes. As soon as they finished, Esther was brought to the room. The scene was precious. She kissed him and spoke to him as though he could hear.

"Peter, you look so handsome," she started. She touched his shoulder and moved her hand down his arm to hold his cold fingers.

"I don't like that you left me so suddenly, without saying goodbye," she said, now softly crying. "But I know you are in a better place, and I will probably be coming soon enough to be with you."

She motioned for the others that were standing in the doorway to come in.

"Come see how peaceful he looks," she said, wiping the tears from her face.

Everyone, including the children, gathered in the bedroom. Some cried, others stood silent.

Then, sure as good has a way of making its way into the face of tragedy, Paul stunned everyone by announcing that he was a licensed preacher and could officiate Peter's funeral. Not that Peter's funeral needed to be officially performed by clergy, for who, in a world gone mad, would care. But his announcement caused great surprise, like a doorbell ringing and your best friend has come to help in a crisis. Paul's ministry was a welcomed contribution.

"It doesn't matter who buries Peter or who says the prayers and recites the Scripture, but I would be honored if you would allow me to do this," his voice cracked as the words came out.

Rachael was stunned. Once again God had covered everything. How convenient it was that someone in the group had ministerial capabilities and could conduct a funeral service.

"I marvel how God has provided," she said, looking around at everyone in the room. "First a doctor, and now we learn that we have a minister among us."

It was two o'clock in the afternoon when Paul gathered the group back together at Peter's bedside and officiated a very simple but meaningful service.

"Death waits for no one," he reminded everyone. "It comes even during Advent."

Indeed, Christmas was just two weeks away.

He read Scripture and prayed. When he finished, Esther spoke of their life and what a good husband he was. They had no children, and that was a welcome relief for Rachael, who would worry that they should be found and notified.

Peter's body was wrapped in white sheets.

The lights were dimmed in the bedroom, and dinner was served at five o'clock, an hour early, so the men could begin digging immediately at dark. It seemed terribly weird and spooky to the children to have a dead body upstairs. Conner and Charles were extremely freaked out, and Stacey and Michael asked questions and made childish comments.

"Keep quiet," Susan told them, while they sat at the dining table. "You shouldn't be talking about Mr. Rubinstein."

Esther placed her teacup carefully onto the saucer and smiled at the children before she began to speak.

"That's all right, Susan, we will let them talk and ask questions. After all, death is a natural thing, and it comes to us all eventually."

No one talked much after that; they just ate and said necessary things, like, "Please pass the salt."

Immediately after dinner, everyone gathered in the grand room while the grave was being dug some two hundred feet beyond the stable, in a wooded area behind the mansion. Maggie stayed close to Esther, speaking to her in soft loving tones as if she could shield the grief that engulfed the poor woman's heart.

The moon was full, and the sky cloudless, allowing the men to see without flashlights. The frost line was only a couple inches deep, due to warm fall temperatures. The men dug silently, making only gestures if they needed to say something.

Rachael left the grand room to look on the scene through the kitchen window. In the shadowy light of the moon she could faintly see the figures of the three men digging the grave. A stabbing surge of sorrow gripped her spirit. I mustn't cry, she thought to herself. *I can't let the others see my sorrow.* She looked toward the sky, heartsick about all that was happening, yet knowing that God was looking down on Carson Hill.

When the grave was deep enough, a plastic drop cloth was spread into the hole for a liner. The men returned to the mansion and carried Peter's body out, carefully placing it into the plastic liner and then wrapping it around Peter's body. No words were spoken. They shoveled the dirt back into the hole and put leaves and dead branches over the site. Snow would cover the grave soon.

******

The presence of Baby Beth had a healing touch on everyone. Her laughter and googling helped to keep anxiety at a manageable level. One life was gone, and a new life was taking form. She was the sunshine and the promise of hope for the future. She was also beginning to be very spoiled. But who gave a guiding thought to that! Beth was the only one who could get by with almost any behavior. In some ways she was envied because she had no fear and knew nothing about the condition of the world. No one cared if Beth was overindulged in or even if she became bratty. And it made no difference to anyone, especially to Rachael, that Beth had been carried in another woman's womb. She was her mother now. And to everyone's delight, this little tyke was growing. So was the romance between Rachael and Kendall.

It seemed fitting that Kendall and Rachael should be married. Why not, now that there was a licensed preacher among them. The festivity of a wedding would bring something good to all of them. But there would be no wedding until Kendall proposed to Rachael.

******

Maggie and Lillian decided that the Christmas tree should come out of the attic and the house decorated as it always was in the past, that is, if Rachael did not object or find it difficult to manage the memories of all the Christmases past on Carson Hill.

"Yes, we will have Christmas," she said. Christmas is the reason we are here together as Believers. Without God sending us a Savior we would have been lost long ago." So, without any further ado, Connie joined their efforts, and the mansion was brimming with tinsel and joy. A stranger looking on might liken their happy spirit to that of lonely soldiers experiencing peace on Christmas Eve on faraway battlefields. The laughter and decorations in the mansion brought a measure of wonderment, so very needed to lift hearts from sadness and worry. In spare moments Rachael sat at the grand piano and played Christmas carols, even the delightful Christmas Song that spoke of chestnuts roasting on an open fire.

In the evenings that followed before Christmas Eve, the entire household gathered in the grand room for songs and stories of how each family celebrated the holiday. Even with the threat of evil and the fear of authorities banging on the door with guns drawn to take them away, there continued the joyous mirth of

Christmas as it made its way to every heart. The children drew pictures of Christmas trees and made gifts out of paper and tape and colored them with crayons. Each day something new was placed under the tree.

Lillian worked hard to stretch the food supply and plan for a special Christmas dinner. It was increasingly more difficult to prepare balanced meals, much less a holiday dinner. She discussed the problem with Kendall, thinking he might be able to get food items from the BBO. He thought it best to wait until after Christmas, even knowing her log revealed there would soon be several shortages in the pantry and freezers. Bartering could not wait much longer.

******

Three days before Christmas Eve, and while the household was gathered in the grand room, breaking news came across the television screen. It was the news they all feared. The BBO underground movement was discovered in Troy by government authorities who were tipped off by a local citizen. The tipster overheard a relative talking about the operation and greedily sold the information to the authorities. Names of the members were disclosed. The news reporter stated that police broke into a secret meeting of the BBO being held in the office of Dr. Luke Saunders. Several underground members were killed, including Dr. Luke. His picture was flashed on the television screen, along with other pictures identifying some of the underground members. Their family members were also killed.

Kendall stood in shock, while Rachael burst into tears and hurried to him. In one horrifying moment, the entire household was swept into an emotional state of panic and hysterical crying.

Martin didn't know what to do with the news. He paced the floor mumbling *God, please help us, please Lord, help us*. Laura gathered her children, trying to shield them from the terror in their father's eyes, while the surge of horror continued to waft its way across the television screen. Karen and Paul quickly moved close to their children, sensing the fear that was engulfing them. Nathan had already bedded down, so Connie got up and moved close to Rose and Esther, putting her arms around them. It was a scene that could only be understood by someone on the battlefield who saw his comrades die from an unexpected grenade explosion.

The discovery of the underground BBO network, and the loss of Kendall's parents, caused enough fear in the mission residents to throw them into a severe depressed psychological state. Reality cannot be masked. Faith, even with all its sustaining attributes, has its momentary limits. Extreme sorrow and fear instantly gripped everyone. Loss of precious lives and dashed hopes of staying safe and having the help of the BBO was like waking from a nightmare only to find it is real. The senseless act of a betraying citizen and the brutal actions of the police force accelerated every emotion that had been kept at bay. Even the smile of baby Beth could not comfort the grief everyone was experiencing. Forget the joy of Christmas; their sorrow crushed it like a ten-ton boulder.

The following morning, Rachael got up early to talk with Maggie and Lillian privately in the kitchen.

"Our state of affairs is as horrible as the day we found Grant shot to death," Rachael said. "In fact, it's worse, because there are hundreds of people already dead, and thousands more that will be killed." Maggie and Lillian agreed while she continued.

"Christmas is only two days away, and we must try to make it happy for the children's sake. We can't let our fear and our grief ruin the children's Christmas, let alone our own lives. We must fight as best we can; we must keep going. We must live as though the children in this house will survive and grow into adulthood."

"You're right," Maggie said. "God and Grant both would want us to keep fighting."

But it seemed their words might just be words with no worth. The fight was huge. The consequences were enormous. Everyone feared the same plight that met the Troy BBO could come to Carson Hill.

"Tonight I want to give a pep talk to the others," Rachael continued. "Maggie, I want you to also speak. You know the heart of the Carsons and the Garrisons, how we have always been survivors and builders. In the past, when I lost my way, you were there to help rescue me. We are needful of your wise counsel and encouragement. You must help me give courage to the others tonight."

She was asking for something Maggie might not be able to do, for the same fear that was raging in everyone's mind was also thundering in hers.

"If only we could ring out the terror and sorrow of this world like we would a dirty ol' dishrag," Maggie said.

Rachael nodded, "We're in the fight of our life. The world has an appointment with kismet, and we cannot save it, and most likely cannot save ourselves."

Maggie was an old lady, but there was a force within her that never failed to catapult her spirit in the right direction. A Divine infilling, as it were, always gave her the right words when they were needed. Tonight she would join with Rachael and say whatever the

Divine Presence compelled her to say. Together, they would encourage the others to replace their fear with confidence in God. He was their only hope.

Lillian did not say a word while Rachael and Maggie talked, but there was plenty going on in her mind and heart. She had been a skeptic, a renegade, a spiritual loss. But in the months that were slipping by she realized that the only hope for her was to believe on the Lord Jesus Christ and be saved. Quietly she made her confession weeks ago without telling Maggie. She couldn't hold it inside any longer.

"I want you to know that I accepted Christ as my Savior," she blurted out, interrupting with absolutely no continuity in what was being said between Rachael and Maggie.

Rachael and Maggie stopped talking and stood like two people startled by a blasting siren. Then came the tears, those wonderful tears of rejoicing. No altar call could match what was happening in that kitchen. The angels in heaven had already sung at Lillian's conversion, but they no doubt were singing again.

******

The evening meal was simple. It consisted of fried spam, canned sliced potatoes that were browned in the same skillets as the spam, canned green beans, V8 Juice, and warm biscuits. Lillian topped it off with a delicious mock apple pie made from Ritz crackers. Weak hot tea was served with the dessert, and chilled reconstituted milk was poured into glass mugs for the children. When the meal was finished, everyone gathered in the grand room as usual. Rachael's pep talk was short and to the point, as though she couldn't wait for Maggie to speak.

The beloved woman stood up and walked to the front of the fireplace. It seemed that she should establish some sort of invisible podium for herself. The backdrop of the fireplace would bring good focus even without flames.

"I read about a man who lived hundreds of years ago," she began. "He was a hard worker like all of you. He held true to his convictions, just as all of us are doing. The authorities nevertheless put him in prison, actually more than once. They flogged him severely and exposed him to death time and time again. Five times he was beaten with thirty-nine lashes. Three times with rods, then stoned and shipwrecked. He suffered from the danger of bandits. He was hungry and thirsty. Yet, in all of this, he found strength and deliverance through the God he loved and served. This man was the Apostle Paul, whose story is recorded in the Scriptures we are well acquainted with. Let me tell you how he managed his life. He did not complain because his journey was not easy, but surprisingly he boasted about his trouble with his adversaries. He was content in his weaknesses and in the insults from others. He had all sorts of persecutions and difficulties. He was strong in all of them. We can be like him.

"Brothers and sisters," she continued, "we belong to the Lord. It is no coincidence that we are together in this place. God has brought us here for this moment in time. We must trust Him, just as Paul trusted Him. We must stand strong and not faint. We have come this far, and we cannot give up. We have committed to do the right thing by keeping ourselves free from the evil that is at work in our world. The journey will now be much harder, but we know the One who is leading us. Let's trust Him and not let fear overtake us."

Finishing her speech, Maggie walked to take her place at the grand piano. Rachael seated herself at the keyboard and began the introduction to the song Maggie had chosen to sing for their inspiration. She lifted her lovely contralto voice to fill the room with the melody and words of "A Mighty Fortress Is Our God."

> "...And tho' this world, with devils filled, Should threaten to undo us;
> We will not fear for God hath willed
> His truth to triumph through us,
> The prince of darkness grim –
> We tremble not for him;
> His rage we can endure,
> For lo his doom is sure, One little word will fell him.
> ...Let goods and kindred go,
> This mortal life also; The body they may kill:
> God's truth abideth still,
> His kingdom is forever."

Paul got up and walked to Kendall. He held his hand out to grab hold of his brother in Christ. It ended in a hug.

"Brother," he said, "I know you are hurting. We all hurt for you. Just know that we love you and we're here for you, for whatever you need."

Kendall shook his head as if to say, yes, I know you're here for me. The rest of the evening seemed to be filled with assuring peace.

******

Before going to bed, Rachael opened her journal to the next empty page. The household was quiet. Sleep would hopefully come to those who needed it most. Although Kendall's heart was broken by the death of his parents, he would be comforted by her love. She would help to fill the empty space his parent's death had suddenly created. She would help to give the love he missed. She and the others would help to fill the void that Peter Rubinstein's death had unexpectedly left in Esther's heart.

Night lights kept the hallways dimly lit and passable. The armed security system gave assurance that an intruder would be heard. Duke curled up on the foot of her bed, as though all was safe and cozy, while Beth slept peacefully in her crib. She set her journal aside and smoothed the blanket around Beth's little shoulders and then touched her lips to her fingers and gently laid them on the baby's forehead. The little one's peaceful sleep was scarcely reassuring; her journey into the future was far from promising. But nevertheless, Rachael felt this child was given to her for a purpose.

In the quiet of the night, while the world reeled in the throes of madness, Rachael's mind moved back to a time when she was a little girl. Like Beth, she had no worries. Her sleep came uninhibited and without effort, as though an angel sprinkled stardust in her eyes every night and gently carried her to a fantasy land of sweet dreams. Those days were gone. Her parents were gone. Almost everything she loved was gone. Freedom was gone. She picked up her pen and wrote the words to a song her grandmother Carson sang long before she knew what the words meant:

> *"Awake, my soul, to joyful lays,*
> *And sing thy great Redeemer's praise;*
> *He justly claims a song for me,*

His lovingkindness, oh how free.
Tho' numerous hosts of mighty foes,
Tho' earth and hell my way oppose;
He safely leads my soul along,
His loving-kindness, oh how strong."

******

A new-fallen snow was blanketing the Irish Hills on Christmas Eve. Rachael and Kendall stood at the grand room windows, watching it dance slowly in the wind and fall to the ground.

"It looks so serene out there," she remarked. "Nature has no inkling that something is terribly wrong. Its' beauty defies evil as though it doesn't exist."

She looked at Kendall, hoping to find comfort in his eyes, but they seemed sad.

"I wish I could grab hold of winter's enchantment and run far away with it," she continued, slipping her arm around Kendall's waist, as they looked out across a wonderland of glistening snow. He remained silent, and she understood. The grief of losing his parents could not be lessened, no matter how beautiful Carson Hill looked, and no matter what she said to him.

"The children are really excited," she said to him.

"I've noticed," he finally answered. "You and Maggie and the others have done a splendid job of creating Christmas for all of us."

He put his arms around her and drew her close. She moved in tight against him and wondered if he felt the same, if he were bursting with desire for her like she was for him. Could she want him simply because she had known the love of another man and wanted to be loved like that again? Was her desire for him because she was afraid? Oh how she wanted him to understand his own intrinsic desires for happiness, and see her as the beautiful catalyst that could ignite his purpose in life.

"I love you, Rachael," he said, startling her thoughts.

What is this, she thought? Suddenly he tells me he loves me. Oh, how I have wanted to hear those words.

"Oh, Kendall, I love you, too, so very much," she whispered.

He kissed her while she waited to hear more words, words like will you marry me, but there was silence.

She would wait for those words, knowing that so often the most wonderful joy in life comes not so much in the having, but in the wanting.

******

The music and words of the song Silent Night filled the mansion. It was Christmas Eve, and the atmosphere was filled with peace. Indeed, it was the peace that passes all understanding. A beautiful crest of new-fallen snow glistened on the frozen lake below the hill. It was as though the world had stopped just long enough to let them have this special night. Rachael set her finest crystal goblets on a silver tray, then filled them with grape juice. She waited in the grand room for the children to exchange their homemade gifts with each other before offering her special gift. There were no expensive perfumes wrapped in shiny paper, or boxes filled with cashmere sweaters, or silk robes, or gold rings. Instead, the gifts were made of paper and tape and the marvelous creativity of children. The spirit around the Christmas tree was better than gold and silver could ever bring. If this was the last Christmas on earth, it was far more special than any they had celebrated before.

Rachael brought the silver tray to the grand room. In the spirit of gift-giving, she set the tray down on the ottoman and began handing each of them a crystal goblet.

"This is my gift to all of you," she said as she passed them around. It was not Holy Communion, but there was something in this special offering that touched every heart. Rachael loved them and served each of them, one by one. It was the finest she had to give, and perhaps the best gift she had ever given on Christmas Eve.

Lillian brought a large bowl of popcorn from the kitchen, followed by Connie, who carried cookies made from packaged cake mix.

This was an unusual, even weird, Christmas Eve when comparing it with those in the past. Paper gifts, strangers, Carson Hill instead of New York City, fear, peace, joy, and death, all mixed together in one pot to produce a Christmas Eve at Carson Hill that would be remembered throughout eternity.

Outside, the evergreens drooped under the weight of the snow. The hillside was white, like wool. The Irish Hills were picturesque, without a hint that the world was ravished with tyranny and oppression.

The snow continued to fall throughout Christmas Day, and their celebration continued with songs and laughter. Peace surrounded everyone like a holy hedge of protection against the horrible fear that gripped their hearts the day the Troy BBO was discovered. Christmas day came to an end with one lasting impression; it was wrapped with joy and tied with happiness.

CHAPTER 7
TO MARKET TO BARTER, TO GET A FAT PIG

MEALS WERE GETTING SLIM WITH less variety. Lillian's concern about the shortages in the pantries and freezers made her fretful. Of course, there was no shortage of complaints when breakfast every morning consisted of oatmeal, reconstituted milk, and a half serving of canned fruit. Flour, biscuit mix, and sugar were getting low enough that she was using those items to enrich just the dinner meals. Canned meat was also getting low. The only food items that were holding out well were the powdered milk, oatmeal, and popcorn. Cooking oil and frozen butter remained plentiful, but without meat for protein and flour for grain, and at least one good serving of fruit each day, their nutrition would soon be poor. It was time for serious bartering.

Lillian consulted with Rachael secretly so as not to call alarm to the serious shortages. What good would that do but make everyone feel guilty about eating. It was time to call the men into the conference and lay before them the food shortage crisis.

Cautiously, Rachael divulged to the men that in the library safe was approximately twenty thousand dollars' worth of jewels and approximately twenty-five thousand dollars in gold watches for bartering. There were also diamonds set in bracelets.

"Independent grocery stores are the ones we must deal with," she soberly told them. "The big chains are held accountable to Chimera. It's risky, but it's time we started bartering for food."

She laid out the plan that she and Grant created when the mission idea first came to them.

"Only one man should go each trip," adding to that comment that they should drive her van rather than Kendall's because her van had a bogus license plate that could not be traced.

"It's safer this way for several reasons, but the main reason is that one man traveling alone reduces the chances of others being caught if something should go wrong. God forbid that anything should happen, but we have to consider this.

It was well known to all of them that police were randomly spot-checking license plates from their patrol cars. Kendall's license plate was logged into Chimera. A trace on it might put more people in trouble in Troy. The name "Saunders" would mean certain interrogation and possibly jail, even death. Therefore, her van stood a better chance of keeping authorities from searching out people who might be connected to Kendall and also keeping the authorities off Carson Hill.

This was sober talk and risky business. The three men gave their consent to everything Rachael proposed.

"I agree, ethnic owned grocery stores would be our best bet," Kendall said, as he looked for confirmation from the other two men.

"There are ways to do this successfully," Martin said. "You can enter the store with one of the watches on your wrist. Strike up a conversation with the owner and show off the watch. If the owner appears interested, then the door is open for bartering. If not, you leave quickly."

"Good thought," Paul said, "and take only enough jewelry to buy what we need, no more. That way, if we get robbed, we only lose so much. If store owners or venders want to coerce or pander us, then we take what we can get and let it go. There's not much benefit in haggling when we need to make deals quickly."

Kendall spoke up, "We could also hit the Eastern Market Place downtown. If we could get some fresh greens, vegetables, and fruits in here, it would stall off using more of our canned goods. The market place would probably be about as safe as an independent grocery store because it is mainly patronized by well-known restaurant owners and probably not policed closely."

"Right," Paul said, laughing, as he brought up the thought that flashed into his mind. "I hear they have livestock down there, so we could bring back a pig if we knew how to slaughter it."

All three men laughed, but Rachael frowned, letting them know she didn't like that suggestion, and this was no time to be joking.

"Let's just stick to what we know we can handle," she said.

They brainstormed a bit longer while Martin logged into the computer and brought on screen the names of the grocery stores in the Detroit area. Then he printed a copy of a Detroit map. They marked and numbered the stores on the map, each according to geographical location and ease of access from the expressway. Each trip would have a designated driver and a designated location—no detours or gallivanting. The whereabouts of the driver was to be slated before he left the mansion. That way, if he did not return, his general whereabouts would be known, and someone could go looking. They would also carry with them the cell phone Kendall bought several months ago.

So it was settled that the men would take turns driving into Detroit to barter for food. The driver would leave early, before the sun was up, in order to be on the expressway with the morning rush. The assumed license plate on Rachael's van was worrisome for them, so the less conspicuous they were, the better. That meant getting into the morning rush hour while still dark and blending in with the traffic. Returning to Carson Hill during the afternoon rush hour would also offer safety. The more traffic, the better.

Kendall would make the first trip because he was more familiar with Detroit than the others. He would carefully case things out while he drove into the city. If he spotted any stores that were not on their list, and they looked good, he would make a mental note of it. When they exhausted Detroit, they would consider Lansing and Jackson.

******

The trip was circumspect, with no unusual problems that put him at risk. His schedule slated him to check out two stores close to downtown on his way in, and then stop at the Eastern Market before returning. It was a lot to accomplish, but if he had success, food worries would be eased for a while.

The van was packed full of food when he started the trip back. Among his bounty were eight bags of fresh turnips greens, each weighing sixteen ounces. These would freeze well. At the same place he carried away ten fifteen-pound bags of Michigan white potatoes. The potatoes could be kept in the cool wine cellar. One of the less expensive watches bought those goods. At another stand, he bartered for red and white cabbages, carrots, apples, and two ten-pound bags of onions.

At the independent grocery stores, he was able to get biscuit mix, Eggbeaters, sugar, and canned tuna fish, along with a few paper products. It was amazing the deals he made with the watches. Gold seemed the best bartering tool they had.

On his way back, he thought about plastic freezer bags for the turnip greens and wondered if Lillian had enough of them. This was not a life or death question, so he opted not to make a call on the cell phone, but rather watch for a small grocery store or party store at a gas station. However, giving a watch for plastic bags seemed a bit senseless. Maybe he could think of something else to make it worth the sale.

Keeping a look-out for a store, he decided that his winter jacket might be a good bartering item, better than a watch. Hopefully, he would find a store and his bargaining chip would work.

Turning onto the service drive, rather than getting involved in expressway traffic, he drove for several miles, watching for a store that might have what he needed. Mile after mile, there was no store that would come close to having plastic freezer bags. There were tobacco stores, nail salons, pizza restaurants, but nothing that sold plastic bags. Thinking he should give up, he was ready to make a right turn back onto the expressway when he spotted a little store next to a dry cleaner. He turned and parked at the shabby curbside.

The store was on the slummy side of town, and it looked as though it might be a front for drugs. Kendall needed to proceed with caution so that the owner didn't get any wrong impressions. The spot he parked in was near the store's front door, which made it easy to get back to the van in a flash if he suspected trouble.

He got out and locked the van, being careful to press the alarm button that would secure the doors. No way did he want to have his precious treasure stolen. When inside the store, he casually said hello to the dark-skinned man behind the counter and looked around. Something was cautioning him to be careful, don't ask for plastic bags. This might make the man think he was after drugs. It might also be misconstrued as a bogus password or catchphrase that would intimidate the man. Instead, he just silently walked around the store, looking for plastic bags. He spotted some disposable plastic containers in the same isle as waxed paper and trash bags. The containers would work as well as plastic bags. No other customers were in the store, so without wasting a second, he gathered up all the containers, six packages in all. Then he walked to the counter, put them down, and took off his jacket. "I'll give you this jacket for these containers," he said to the man.

The man looked at the containers and then at the jacket. He examined the jacket closely, then laid it down on the counter and picked up one of the container packages, and put it with the jacket, saying, "Just five packages and you got a deal."

Kendall nodded approvingly, picked up the five packages of disposable containers, and left.

It was cold without his jacket, but the heater in the van kept him comfortable. *Boy, what a day* he said to himself, feeling like he was Santa Claus without the reindeer. He knew the women would be all over him with hugs for what he was bringing home.

******

News reports were of extreme importance now that the underground networks were being destroyed. The cable news network was constantly aired in the grand room.

Laura was picking up magazines that were left on the couch when a news bulletin come through reporting a significant earthquake in California. It was serious. She immediately gathered the others.

Facts were sketchy at first, but as the television network kept in touch with their reporters in the area, details started coming in. Everyone stopped what they were doing and assembled quickly in the grand room. The news traveling off the widescreen was hair-raising.

"We're just now getting reports that an earthquake measuring 9.2 on the Richter scale has crossed portions of California and traveled into the state of Nevada," the news anchor said. *"There are some reports indicating that the coastline of California, from Santa Rose northward down to Santa Barbara, which is just north of Los Angeles, has separated, or broken off. We don't know how far inland the separation is at this moment. The quake apparently took an 'L' shaped pattern from what we're hearing."*

Everyone was astounded, as well as being markedly unnerved. Long ago, during their studies of the Scripture in Revelation, Rachael and Grant knew that the world would see great earthquakes, and by great, they meant gargantuan. Of course, they could not predict when they were coming, but their research on the fault lines across the US, and their study of biblical prophecy, fully convinced them that something of this magnitude was coming.

Citizens with cell phones were videotaping the scenes and sending the pictures to the cable news networks. Dozens of videos were pouring into the newsrooms across the nation.

"It's unbelievable," Paul commented. "Look at that!" The network showed the scene from a helicopter. "The coastline of California looks like tiny islands."

It was a grueling scene: massive destruction along miles of coastline. Esther and Rose were so overcome that they had to sit down, while the others felt their nerves shiver.

"*We have a report from one of our affiliates in Oakland,*" the newscaster announced.

The station quickly switched to the reporter.

"*This is Ted Prescott in Oakland,*" the reporter began. "*I am standing near what used to be Interstate 101 that runs from the Coastal Ranges to Los Angeles. There's nothing left of it. It's gone, cracked into millions of large chunks of pavement. It's an incredible sight. The cars that were traveling on this Interstate are crushed in the crevasses, or missing entirely. Let's pan over to the area.*"

The cameraman panned across a row of half-buried cars, which obviously had people inside. The scene was nauseating. The reporter continued after he directed his cameraman to pan the ocean side and zoom in as close as possible.

"*You can see in the distance small pieces of land that resemble tiny islands,*" the reporter continued. "*These land fragments are the coastline. The earthquake apparently tore the beaches away from the mainland.*"

With that said, the camera view shook as a huge aftershock occurred.

Everyone kept listening and watching while the horror of the massive earthquake unfolded on the television screen.

"I remember reading about a futurist who claimed that a reconstruction of the US would take place through a series of earthquakes,"

Kendall quickly added, noting in his recollection that the person failed the litmus test on being accurate one hundred percent with every prediction he made. Nonetheless, this futurist's predictions were interesting to read. It appeared that the futurist made a home run on this earthquake prediction.

Kendall was referring to a noted futurist who was popular in the early nineteen hundreds, touting beguiling, mysterious predictions. He claimed to have the gift of healing and prophecy. He gave readings from trance-like states of consciousness, 14,000 readings in all. As his so-called gift increased, he began reporting snapshots of the future that predicted the 1929 fall of the Stock Market, just a few months before it happened. His imagination was quite wild and sometimes mysteriously correct.

He predicted the dates of the Second World War. In one sleep-trance, he revealed detailed information about ancient Egypt. He stated that a chamber would be found under the front paws of the Great Sphinx. He foretold that in these chambers, the records of an ancient civilization would be found, a civilization that inspired the entire Egyptian culture. These ancient people were called Atlantis.

This man was correct on some projections and incorrect on others. Kendall knew that seers are interesting, but only God's Holy Word predicts the future for mankind.

Yet most interesting to Kendall was his recollection of this man's prediction that a foreshadowing upheaval of the eastern portion of America, and the greater portion of Japan, would fall into the sea. New York, Los Angeles, and San Francisco would all be destroyed and become the bed of the ocean. These events were yet to be seen, but nonetheless, they were interesting meditations coming from someone who occasionally was correct.

What the group on Carson Hill was watching unfold on the television was not this long ago prediction. Interesting as the predictions were, this mammoth earthquake was not accurately foreseen by this soothsayer who lived a hundred years ago.

"Well, there's been plenty of speculation and many predictions down through the years, but this looks like the real thing, straight out of the Bible," Rachael said.

Esther and Rose had seen and listened to enough. It was far too much for them. They left the room, while the rest could not tear themselves away from the gruesome scenes. Thousands were presumed dead. Homes by the scores were destroyed. Many areas were impassible even by foot. The news continued, taking over the regularly scheduled programs.

This appeared to be "the big one" Californians were hoping would never come, but it wasn't over yet.

Another earthquake was felt in the mid-west, in the Des Moines area. Large crevasses opened up, and basins were formed from its power. Much of the Des Moines River was gobbled into the earth. It was incredible, as though God was pouring out His wrath. The river was missing from Ft. Dodge to the border of Illinois.

In the long hours of the night, the group watched the news reports, feeling as though they were watching a science fiction thriller, only instead of monsters destroying the earth, the earth was destroying itself.

LILLIAN AND CONNIE PREPARED BREAKFAST as usual. Those who stayed up most of the night were tired and emotionally exhausted. The silence at the table was heavy. The reality of fulfilled prophecy was unquestionable. Their awareness of the Revelation Scriptures convinced all of them that everything they were seeing and experiencing, both from the government and by way of natural disaster, was a fulfillment of the end-times. How many days, months, even years the entire pandemonium would go on was unknown. Depending upon where prophecy literally begins, it could go on for years, or it could end immediately. Prayers were said around the table for the injured as well as those who were on searches for their loved ones.

There was an immediate change in the morale of most Americans, and it was no different with those who lived at the mansion. The US was vulnerable, too weakened now to be concerned about any global enemies. The result of Chimera, as well as the earthquakes, convinced everyone on Carson Hill that human behavior is grossly predictable whenever there are calamities. People either start thinking about God, or they poke Him in the eye. The result of this present situation was worse than what took place on September 11, 2001. This present catastrophe was harboring a higher level of fear because it was terrifyingly widespread and involved thousands more. The California quake definitely could be labeled as "the big one." Hundreds were becoming distraught, some even committing suicide, while others blamed God and waxed cold.

Looting and crime elevated, making the entire scene throughout the country look as though something had been loosed from hell. Local and national news stations confirmed that no one was safe on the streets, even in places not affected by the quakes. Ticker tapes running across the bottom of the television screen announced that the nation-wide Security Alert was bumped up to red.

The Secretary of Safety recommended that people avoid the streets as much as possible. Chimera's promise of peace and prosperity was totally destroyed in the face of this natural disaster. Could the government regain its power and keep the masses under control? That was the question asked on Carson Hill. Rachael's belief was that a forced global financial and military system could not solve the problems. The system had no power to comfort. Tyranny would continue.

******

Far and away Rachael's thoughts carried her as she lay on her bed, waiting for sleep to come. The Sovereign God was in control, but the world was caught in the throes of disaster.

As night fell upon the Irish Hills, the mansion was once again quiet. The security system was armed, the lights were dimmed, and everyone was in their rooms; most were already asleep. The earthquake events had taken its psychological toll on all of them, including the children. No one watched the sensational newscasts and saw the terrible destruction of life and property without becoming morbidly depressed. Rachael thought about her parents, Walter and Catherine. She wished they could be here to put their arms around her. She thought about Grant. She remembered his strength and his love for her. She remembered how wonderful their marriage had been. The good days were gone now. Even being in love with Kendall, it seemed to her that she was living in a nightmare where someone flipped a switch, and suddenly she was in a cold, evil world with no way of escape. Like the words of a popular song years ago, the days of wine and roses had laughed and run away.

Although she knew that her mission was set to save a small remnant of good people, people who had come to her mansion for safety and shelter, she wished there was some way to bring back the good days. She loved Kendall, and he was filling much of the void in her empty heart, but still she cherished Grant's memory. In many respects, her love for him would never die. She deliberately imagined his face and his touch. *Is it possible*, she asked herself, *to love two men?*

The night would be sleepless thanks to her restless thoughts and accelerating world conditions, especially the chaos prevailing across the US. The country was in an upheaval, worse than imaginable with two great earthquakes. The catastrophe was affecting the Stock Markets and the entire world. There was no peace anywhere in the world. Instead of peace in the US, the nation had nothing but misery and hopelessness. The safety of each person living in the mansion was of immediate concern. Restless and tossing, she sensed they were becoming more vulnerable now that people were scattered from their homes, many having no place to go. She worried if bartering could still be accomplished in view of the increasing anarchy. Although Michigan was not directly affected by the earthquakes, the backlash from them was creating widespread terror. She thought about the wine cellar, the place she considered a safe hideaway when she was a kid. Could it possibly be made into a secure place for them to hide? Perhaps it could serve as a temporary hideout where they could escape intruders.

She lay there in the darkness thinking. The wine cellar could hold all of them, including sleeping bags and food for several days. The only drawback was that it was not hidden. It was merely a room built within the basement. Rachael wondered how difficult it would be to camouflage it. Could the men build something around it that would hide it so it would be completely safe during a raid? If so, where would they get the lumber? How long would it take to build it? A thousand thoughts and questions raced through her mind as she contemplated how she would keep everyone safe. The night hours moved slowly as she thought and prayed. They must do something more than simply keep the drapes drawn and the lights dimmed at night. The security system was nothing more than an alarm. Finally, she decided that she would address the idea of camouflaging the wine cellar into a temporary haven at breakfast in the morning.

A couple of hours before dawn, she closed her eyes and drifted off to sleep.

CHAPTER 8
THE GRAND ROOM

MORNING CAME, AND WITH IT another day to be thankful Carson Hill remained safe. The Irish Hills remained peaceful and quiet, with brilliant sunlight cascading over the rolling knolls like aerobic waves rising and falling in rhythmic tempo. The physical structure of the mansion was basically hidden behind trees and large evergreens. However, people living in the homes and cottages surrounding the lake below, and those driving on the road that circled the shoreline, could see the lights at night in the mansion. The place was decades old and well known to those who lived along the lake, and no one paid attention to it. Most people simply thought it was unoccupied much of the time. However, in the restless thoughts and worries that kept Rachael awake most of the night, she considered the attraction the lights in the mansion presented at night. At breakfast, she addressed every thought and every precaution.

The low lighting at night in the hallways and throughout the first floor of the mansion would be eliminated. Every bedroom after dark would be lit only by the night lights plugged into the wall sockets. Necessary trips to the bathroom would be made in the dim light.

There were emergency flashlights stored in the basement. Those would be brought up and placed in each bedroom.

"I know this makes it more difficult to get around after dark," Rachael said while everyone continued with their breakfast, "but the threat of being found is extremely great now.

"In view of the danger, the sacrifice of turning the lights out will not be too great. Another advantage would be the savings gained in electrical costs. This would slow down the draw on the escrow account at the electric company," she concluded.

"I believe that's a great idea," Martin said, as everyone nodded in agreement. "We can still enjoy the grand room together in the evenings with the dimmer switch turned to basic candlelight brightness."

Fearing that it was only a matter of time before the authorities found a reason to come knocking at the mansion doors, Rachael decided that everyone should remain on the first floor during the daytime hours so they were not scattered all over the house. Children should not be separated from their parents. Her rule was also based on the fact that the less scattered everyone was, the quicker their complete exit would be to the basement.

"Each person, after showering and dressing in the morning, will come downstairs for breakfast, bringing with them whatever they need for the day," she instructed. "Naps for the elderly and Beth will be taken in the grand room, or in the library. Regular medications will be brought to the kitchen and placed in a designated cabinet. No one should go upstairs during the day without permission.

"Maggie and Lillian also will not be going up to their servant quarters on the third floor during the day. The only reason that someone would remain upstairs will be if they are sick and need to be quarantined."

The drills to run to the cellar would continue, and each day the password knock, three knocks followed by two knocks, would be recited and rehearsed so that it was not forgotten. No one was to open the doors unless the password knock was heard.

Preparation for bedtime would begin before dusk, with lights out as soon as it was dark, and only dim light in the grand room and kitchen when necessary.

"All of us will gather after dinner in the grand room for fellowship."

Lillian poured more coffee while Rachael continued.

"I think we should consider building a camouflaged wall around the wine cellar. If authorities come to the mansion, we can hide there. It's a perfect place if the shelves are removed."

She glanced at them to study their reaction. Paul quickly commented.

"Well for sure, if we simply run to the basement to hide, we would be found immediately," he said. "I think we should consider this."

Martin put his coffee cup down, wiped his mouth with his napkin, and spoke, "It will take some brainstorming, but we can do it."

Rachael's confidence was mounting. Concealing the wine cellar and making it into a hideaway gave her the assurance she lacked. But was it as safe as they all imagined?

******

The grand room continued to be the gathering place after dinner each evening, with drapes drawn tight, lights dimmed, and everyone ready for bed. Cleanup in the kitchen was done quickly with the help of Karen. The dinner hour was moved a half-hour earlier to give as much time in daylight to prepare for the evening.

******

Rose was talkative on this particular evening. Perhaps her silent fear of being taken into custody by the authorities made her think of her happy childhood, or maybe it was the sight of Beth peacefully sleeping on Rachael's lap that prompted her memories. Whatever it was that conjured up her thoughts, she began to talk.

"My childhood summers are very memorable to me tonight," she said.

"Tell us about them," Rachael encouraged.

"Well," Rose began slowly, clearing her throat, "On a hot summer's night, when not a breeze would blow to cool our house, the low hum of a fan could lull my sister, Bertha, and I to sleep, as sound asleep as Beth is now in her mother's lap. In the daytime, the buzz of a fly on the screened door was like a symphony. Funny, how simple things like that have a way of bringing peace. I mean, the atmosphere was so quiet we could hear the buzz of a fly.

Everyone was listening, wondering where she was going with this simple, rather unassuming talk.

"The soft clanging of the Venetian blinds at the open windows was a rhythmic sound that made me feel calm and peaceful back then. It was a time when there was peace in the neighborhoods, and no one was locking their doors. A glass of cold water from the refrigerator was one of the best treats of the day. There was no chaos. The world was quiet."

She paused and looked around the dimly lit room to find everyone was looking at her, waiting for her to continue.

"If by some wonderful miracle my sister Bertha and I could sell some scrap to the junkman ridding down the alley in his dilapidated pick-up truck, we might have the good fortune to buy an ice cream cone.

"Ice cream was peddled on three-wheeled bikes back then, you know, bikes that had a large insulated box affixed to the frame. The box was filled with dry ice to keep frozen treats solid. If we missed the ice cream man, then Bertha and I would walk to the corner store and buy a cold soda pop. A nickel back then would buy a soda or an ice cream."

Most were listening politely to Rose's chatter, but some, like Connie and Karen, couldn't help the yawns that accompanied their disinterest in an era they had not experienced, and frankly found rather boring compared to computers and smartphones. Esther, however, nodded whenever she related to some of the things Rose was saying.

"We were poor back then," Rose continued. "It was feast or famine in our kitchen. Either we had plenty, or my mother was rationing. When we feasted, I enjoyed things like liverwurst sandwiches smothered with mustard and cucumber slices. My favorite dessert was chocolate cookies dunked in cold milk. For supper, Mother often cooked spaghetti noodles and mixed them with browned hamburger and tomato soup. It was a simple meal, yet so good. I mean, there I was, a kid growing up in a blue-collar area of Detroit enjoying the simplest things while the elites in the fashionable Grosse Pointe area were eating their T-bone steaks and carving their crowned pork roasts. Bertha and I were basically raised on bread and butter and cheap goulash. But you know, not knowing that there were others who lived far better than I didn't matter one iota."

"How's that?" Connie interrupted. "I don't see how anyone could be that happy about being poor."

Connie's interruption was typical of her generation. The lucrative society that she had just come out of was egocentric and self-interested.

"Well," Rose continued, "Being poor made me ignorant of the finer things others enjoyed. What I mean is, my segregation from the upper class was like an armor that shrouded me from the reality of being quite poor. I didn't know I was poor because I had nothing to compare it to. That wonderful obliviousness gave me a good sense of normalness.

"Bertha and I might have been the least of the common among our peers at school, but the majority of them were not much better off than we were, from a happiness standpoint. There was not a great deal of wealth and prosperity back then. Many of us never knew the difference between liverwurst and expensive *pâté de foie gras*, nor had any of us ever heard of *vichyssoise*, let alone taste it."

"What is that stuff?" Susan interrupted.

Rose laughed as she answered, "*Pâté* is made of the cooked livers from specially fattened geese that are mashed into a paste and served on crackers. *Vichyssoise*, on the other hand, is a creamy French potato and onion soup, usually served cold."

"Yuck!" Susan blurted out.

Rose's reference to these fine foods let everyone know that the woman, although poor as a child, had gained the class and sophistication she had missed growing up. Certainly, her esteemed role as a retired English teacher and community figure, witnessed of her elegance now.

Rose concluded.

"What really mattered back then was that I came to love the good things I knew, and they were as fitting to me as caviar was to the rich."

Laura immediately jumped in on that comment, "That is really interesting, Rose, and very appropriate for us right now, as we are struggling with the loss of our homes and dealing with food shortages and the fear of being found out. We are learning to love the good things we have now."

"Exactly!" Esther pipped up, looking at the children, and directing her comments straight to them.

"You children need to understand that the richness of your lives is not based on whether or not you live in a big house, or have lots of toys, or eat all the things you love. No, your richness comes from having loving parents and living in this beautiful mansion right now, far away from the mean streets of the city."

A good point of view came into being that evening. It was simple and well said, and a clear acknowledgment that their existence was to be cherished, and appropriately their thankfulness would yield them to accept the circumstances in which they found themselves. Indeed, Rose's simple but profound exchange of views brought a new dimension to their evening conversation, and it seemed to catch on. Every night afterward something wonderful was said by someone that brought a true sense of purpose and peace. Everyone, including the children, were learning things they would take with them the rest of their lives, however long that might be.

******

The men confiscated as many boards as possible from the old stable, without tearing it down or making it look like someone recently pillaged it. Their plan was to build a wooden wall across the wine cellar that would resemble a foundation wall. At the same location as the original door on the cellar, an undetectable door was built into the wall. Paul found some whitewash paint that had been stored in the basement by painters who worked at the mansion a few years ago. The wall was rubbed with dirt to make it look old after it was painted.

The wine shelves were torn down and made into benches, just wide enough to accommodate a person sitting or lying down. Bottled water and packaged food provisions were stored under the benches, enough for three days. The men forgot nothing. A five-gallon pail with a tight lid was placed in one corner with a plastic shower curtain tacked to the ceiling for privacy. This would serve as a porta potty. One measured gallon of water was poured into the pail. Disinfectant and tissue were stored in that same corner. Other items included two flashlights, in the event the electricity was disconnected, plus a battery-operated radio, blankets, pillows, paper towels, reading material, crayons, notebooks, and basic first aid items, including a three-day supply of routine medications for Rose and Esther. Rachael brought diapers for Beth and plastic bags for disposal.

Martin adjusted the thermostat so that the internal temperature would be kept at seventy degrees. He replaced the light bulbs with new ones and placed a screwdriver and pliers in a small box beneath one of the benches. A few small holes were drilled through the outer wall for ventilation.

Kendall found large cardboard boxes stuffed with old memorabilia in the attic. He poured the contents out and cut them flat to make a barrier on top of the cement floor. He found an old oriental rug rolled up and tied with yarn in one of the dark corners of the attic. He swept it clean and placed it over the cardboard to provide more insulation over the cement.

Once the cellar cubby was completed and stocked, practice drills started that timed how long it took to get everyone inside. There was concern about the children having fear dashing to the cellar, so the drill became a game with a prize for every child once they reached the cubby.

As the days passed and the drills continued, everyone moved quickly and became comfortable in the hiding place. Who in their wildest imaginations would ever have thought their days would be spent dashing to a cellar hideout and fearing for their lives?

******

It was Kendall's turn again to barter. Lillian needed sugar, raisins, rice, onions, canned soups, and canned meat. An independent grocery store near the Cultural Center in the heart of Detroit had an owner who was agreeable to barter with them. Paul had previously bartered, and the grocer happily took the watches offered without haggling. Bartering was tricky business, but this grocer seemed to be a good person to deal with, obviously because he had customers for the watches. Kendall had great hopes that he could get the things Lillian needed, and meals would remain nutritious. Maintaining good nutrition was extremely important to ward off illness. Kendall knew that stress is handled much better on a full stomach.

Considering what was on the list, Rachael decided that one 14-carat gold eighteen-inch chain and a diamond tennis bracelet, both worth about four hundred dollars, would be plenty to pay. She suggested that Kendall offer the gold chain first. If the store owner hesitated, then he could throw in the diamond bracelet. The jewelry was taken out of their original boxes so they would appear as stolen goods, which oddly enough would make the deal more intriguing.

At seven o'clock the next morning, he finished eating an early breakfast and left the mansion for the Motor City. The streets had settled into a measurable amount of law and order since the earthquake mayhem. Although it was still risky to venture into the metropolitan area, it was not impossible to go there and get back without trouble, if great caution was taken.

The hour and thirty-minute drive to Detroit was well known to him. He was at ease with the familiarity and was actually enjoying the venture. Traffic was heavy, but he reached the entrance ramp of the expressway from the two-lane country road in good time. He eased the van into the slow-moving lane, hoping it would blend well with the other vehicles. No one in the passing cars suspected that he was a defector, driving a van with assumed license plates, much less that he was on his way to barter for food. But there he was, a rebel of the government, a doctor without a practice, hiding out in the Irish Hills of Michigan, on a country knoll called Carson Hill, and in love with the owner of the mansion. Could life get any more intriguing?

It was nine o'clock when he reached the store. Clouds had given way to sunshine, making this cold February day quite pleasant. He parked at the side of the store, near a loading door where cases of canned goods and boxes of food items could be easily carried out and put into the van. The owner was perched behind the counter when Kendall opened the door and walked into the store.

"Hey, how's it going?" the man asked.

"Pretty good, how about yourself?" Kendall replied as he walked up to the counter.

The man was wearing a white soiled butcher apron. His hair was slicked back with mousse, and he smelled of cheap shaving lotion.

His high forehead made his eyes look small and beady. He appeared heavier than the description Paul had given.

Three female customers were busy shopping in the narrow aisles. Kendall didn't consider them to be threatening, so he dug in his pocket and showed the owner the list of food he wanted. The man studied it for a while. Then he looked up at Kendall and said, "You got Chimera ID for this stuff?"

Kendall glanced around the store to be sure the women were not in eyeshot. Feeling safe, he pulled the gold chain out of his jacket pocket and laid it down on the counter in front of the man. The grocer examined it carefully.

"Okay, you got a deal, but only ten pounds of sugar, not twenty, and eight boxes of rice, not ten."

Kendall nodded. He walked with the grocer to the back room, where the man's son was lazily mulling around, smoking what smelled like pot.

"Here," his father said, shoving the list into the son's chest. "Get these things together and help this man load them. Only ten pounds of sugar and eight boxes of rice."

The young man faltered back from the strong shove his father gave him. He took a couple of long drags on his cigarette, pinched it with his fingers, and stuck it in his pocket, then slowly started gathering the cases of canned goods on the list. Kendall helped. Sugar, rice, raisins, canned meat, and onions, it was all there, and he was grateful to get it. They worked for only a few minutes getting everything gathered and put into the van. The young man seemed rather anxious for some reason, as though he were expecting someone.

As soon as the van was loaded, the fellow walked quickly back to the store's loading door and slammed it shut behind him. Kendall thought that was strange but went on with his business of closing the van's doors.

He walked to the driver's side and reached for the door handle just as two strange fellows quickly approached him.

"Get in the back," one of the thugs said, shoving a handgun into Kendall's stomach.

He hesitated for a moment but realized the person meant business, especially when he saw the other thug with an open switchblade. He opened the side door and climbed onto the seat. The hoodlum with the gun hopped into the driver's seat, while the other one ran around the front of the van and jumped into the passenger seat.

"What's going on, and what do you want?" he shouted at them.

"Shut up!" the fellow in the driver's seat said, as he peeled out and onto the street. He was wearing a dirty baseball cap set backward on his head. His sleeveless down-filled vest was dirt-spotted. Kendall caught glimpses of his face in the rear-view mirror and guessed his age at somewhere in the twenties.

"I want to know where you are taking me and what you're doing," Kendall said firmly.

"Look mister, my big brother said shut up," the other thug bellowed.

He guessed the second fellow to be about eighteen or nineteen years old. He had short black unkempt hair and was wearing a waist-length leather jacket.

The van peeled down residential streets, going toward the downtown area. They were purposely taking side roads to avoid traffic.

"Look, guys, I don't know what you want, but I don't have anything but these groceries," Kendall told them.

"Ya, and we're the jolly green giant," the driver said.

They both laughed, while the one riding in the passenger seat fumbled with the switchblade as if to scare Kendall.

They turned into a neighborhood where half the houses were boarded up. Kendall was careful to catch some of the street names, so he could find his way out.

They pulled up to a small shabby bungalow and parked near the rear, toward the backyard.

"Get out!" one of them said.

With the gun pointing at his back ribs through the driver's vest, Kendall followed the other fellow up the narrow sidewalk and into the decrepit house. Once they were inside, he was shoved to a couch and told to stay there.

"Okay, Marty, now what?" the younger fellow said, revealing his brother's name.

Marty took off his vest and swung around to shout at Kendall.

"Jimmy and me know you got loot somewhere, and we want it," he said with a tough voice.

"Ya, you'd better fork it over, or you're dead meat," Jimmy said in an effort to back up his brother.

"I don't have any loot," Kendall answered firmly.

"Where you takin' all those groceries anyway?" Marty asked. "You got some sort of hideaway somewhere?"

Kendall knew he would have to be shrewd in order to convince these two thugs that he was not rich and that he was not hiding out somewhere.

"Look guys," he said with an appealing voice, "I help out at that soup kitchen down on Skid Row, you know, the one where they give the homeless bums food and let them spend the night if it's real cold?"

The two thugs looked at each other with a deadpan glance, as if they might believe him.

"All that food is for the soup kitchen," Kendall went on. "They send someone every few days to load up on food to feed those poor homeless fools that roam the streets downtown. I guess the government feels sorry for them."

He was lying through his teeth, and he hoped God would forgive him, but there was no way he was going to let these thugs find out about the mission in the Irish Hills.

"Go out and search the van, Jimmy, see if he's lying," Marty ordered.

Marty then frisked Kendall but did not feel the diamond bracelet in the hidden inner pocket.

These two thugs were not what Kendall considered bright, by any means. Their silly laughter and language marked them as two burnouts trying to play the gangster role.

Jimmy came back into the house and said there was nothing in the van but groceries.

"Maybe he's tellin' us the truth," Jimmy said. "Maybe we got us a real dud."

Marty pulled a cigarette out of his pocket and lit it. He took a few drags and sat down on a grubby upholstered chair across from the couch. He kept his eyes on Kendall while he puffed the cigarette, looking as though he were trying to figure him out. "You leveling with us?" he asked point-blank.

"Ya, I'm tellin' you the truth," Kendall said, trying to sound like them. "I just make runs for the soup kitchen. I don't have no loot."

"What's your name, anyway?" Jimmy asked.

"Bill." That was the quickest name that came to his mind.

"Well, Bill," Jimmy continued, "Sammy will be here tomorrow, so you better not be lying." With that said, he flipped on the television in the corner of the small room and walked out, returning with a rope. He tied Kendall's hands together in front and then tied his ankles together.

"Don't get any ideas about leaving because I will blow your brains out."

Kendall tried to look unshaken, but he was consumed with despair. Rachael and the others were expecting him back in just two hours. They would be frantic with fear wondering where he was and what had happened. He thought about the diamond bracelet, still in the pocket of his jacket. *I'd better not divulge this unless it looks like I'm not going to escape,* he thought.

A weather report flashed across the screen while Jimmy was clicking to different channels. It would be above freezing tonight. *That's one good thing I can be thankful for; the food in the van won't freeze,* he thought.

******

It was four o'clock in the afternoon when everyone at the mansion began to seriously worry about Kendall.

"Did he take his cell phone?" Karen asked, looking at Rachael.

"I'm not sure, but usually he takes it wherever he goes, so I'm sure he has it," Rachael replied.

"Well, maybe he had car trouble, or got tied up in traffic due to an accident and hasn't had a chance to call," Martin said.

Just then, Maggie came walking into the room, holding Kendall's cell phone.

"Look!" she said, "He forgot to take his cell phone."

"I think we should go looking for him," Rachael said. Her concern was obvious. The men were always back by two o'clock when they went into Detroit.

"I think you're right," Paul said. "Let Karen and me go, and we'll backtrack his route and watch for any sign of the van broken down along the road."

"Martin should stay here," Paul quickly added. "We need to have at least one man on the premises all the time."

Everyone agreed.

"That will put you back here around nine o'clock tonight," Rachael said. "I don't like the idea of any of us out at that hour, let alone being in Detroit, but we've got to find Kendall. We are also taking a big risk by driving his van." Her voice was filled with anxiety. She was smothering it the best she could for everyone's sake, but it was obvious she was frightened for Kendall.

It was dark when Paul and Karen reached the city limits of Detroit. All the way in, they watched the roadsides for signs of Kendall and the van but saw nothing. When they drove into the parking lot of the grocery store, the place was closed. There were no cars parked anywhere near the store. They drove down several of the surrounding streets but saw no sign of the van or Kendall.

"We'll head back and watch the road again," Paul said to Karen while dialing the cell phone to inform the others at the mansion. Karen swallowed the lump in her throat, holding back tears.

"Maybe we missed him as he turned onto the road when we were turning off," she said hopefully.

On the way back to the Irish Hills, she kept wishfully thinking aloud, and it helped to keep their hopes up, but there was no sign of Kendall or the van.

Throughout the night, after Paul and Karen reported back to the Irish Hills, Rachael could think of nothing else but the man she loved. She was concerned that something horrible had happened to him. The memories of Grant's murder flooded her mind. Remembering the morning she and Maggie found him slumped over the steering wheel in the garage of their Dearborn condo brought back terrifying feelings. The weeks of grief and the emptiness came back, as though it had never left. *I can't bear for this to happen again,* she thought.

She turned her flashlight onto Beth, peacefully asleep in her crib and oblivious to the fear and panic in her mother's heart. *What will become of this little girl, in a world so terror driven and lost,* she thought. *What will become of me and the rest of these people who are depending on the safety this hillside mansion is giving them? If Kendall never comes back, it will be as though I have met the face of doom and hopelessness again.*

She turned the flashlight on her watch. It was one o'clock in the morning. Completely worn out with fear, she slipped into bed.

"Please God bring Kendall back home," she prayed.

******

It was almost daylight when Kendall woke up on the couch. He felt stiff from lack of movement. The ropes were tight, and his hands were swollen. Jimmy was half asleep in the chair across the room. The gun was still on the table next to him. He and Marty had taken turns in the chair, while the other snoozed in the bedroom down the hallway. Jimmy made sure Kendall knew he would get shot if he tried anything. Once during the night, he put the gun to Kendall's head and laughed.

"What time is it?" Marty said, entering the room.

Jimmy woke up, stretched, and looked at his watch.

"It's almost seven o'clock. Sammy should be here in a few minutes."

"I'm starving," Marty bellowed. "How 'bout you take that van and go get us something to eat?

"Sounds like a good idea to me," Jimmy said, slipping into his jacket.

He jingled the van keys in Kendall's face as if to rub it in that he was going to drive his van.

In just a few minutes, he came back with three breakfast sandwiches and three coffees. Kendall was grateful that he was allowed to eat. It had been twenty-four hours since his last meal. He managed to eat with his hands tied together.

Before he had time to finish his coffee, the third thug they called Sammy drove up in an old jalopy and parked in front of the house. Kendall was watching through the dirty picture window. The thug pushed the rusty car door open with both hands, got out, and sauntered up the short walkway to the front door. It was too dark for him to make out what he looked like through the window, but his frame was large. The hoodlum opened the door and walked in. Kendall stared at him in shock. It was the grocer's son.

"You get any loot from this guy?" Sammy blurted out without greeting his two partners.

Kendall figured it was over now. Sammy seemed smarter than the two thugs who kidnaped him, and he might not believe his story about working in the soup kitchen downtown.

"Nah, we didn't get nothin' from him," Marty said, sipping the last of his coffee.

Sammy walked over to Kendall and struck him in the face.

"You got loot, how else would you be able to buy all those groceries from my Dad," Sammy yelled at him.

Kendall cringed back into the couch, feeling the sting from the blow. But in spite of the wallop on his face, he had picked up a cue from Sammy when he asked how he bought all those groceries. He wouldn't have asked that question if he had suspected a bartered deal. He knew he had better think of something quick before Sammy decided to kill him.

"Look," Kendall said, as he straightened up from the blow. "I just drive a van for the soup kitchen and buy foodstuff for them when they need it."

He looked straight at Sammy, trying to get an inkling of whether or not he believed his story. He continued.

"I gave the soup kitchen's ID to your dad for all that stuff you helped me load into the van. But I do have a diamond bracelet that I stole off an old drunk down at the kitchen. Here, you can have it. It's inside my jacket."

He nodded his head toward his pocket, instructing Sammy to get it.

Sammy reached into the jacket pocket, pulled out the diamond bracelet, and studied it hard.

"It's a good one," Kendall said. "I think it might be worth several hundred dollars. That's why I swiped it."

Sammy examined the bracelet more closely.

"I can get more," Kendall said quickly. "Some guys come in with nice lookin' watches that they probably stole. There are all kinds of stuff on those skid row bums."

Sammy slipped the diamond bracelet into his pocket. "You better not be puttin' me on, man," he said.

"I ain't puttin' nobody on," Kendall said back to him, mimicking Sammy's style of talking. "Let me go, and the next time I come to your dad's grocery store, I'll have something for you—something really nice."

He hated that he was lying again, but there was no way he was going to get out alive unless he did. *Please forgive me, God.*

"We gonna let this guy go," Sammy said to the other two. Then he looked back at Kendall, "But when you come back you better have somethin' good for all three of us, you hear? Else next time I see you at my Dad's store, you'll wish you had."

He took his finger and drew it across his throat, letting Kendall know that he would slit his throat if he didn't come up with some good loot next time. Kendall figured these guys were hooked on dope and they stole to get their fix.

"Ya, man, I hear you, and I'll bring you somethin' real good," Kendall said, as Sammy untied the rope around his hands and ankles.

Jimmy threw the van keys at him and said, "Get lost."

Kendall caught the keys and was out the door in a flash.

CHAPTER 9
THE WEDDING

LILLIAN WAS BUSY TIDYING UP the kitchen when three knocks, followed by two more, sounded on the door. She paused, wondering if she heard correctly. Then three more knocks, followed by two. She carefully peeked around the door curtain, thinking that although the knocks were correct, she must see who it was before she unarmed the security system and opened the door.

"Oh, my land, it's Kendall," she screamed as she caught a glimpse of the tall, handsome figure standing there. Without a second's delay, she disarmed the security system and threw the door open.

Hearing the commotion, Maggie and Susan hurried into the kitchen, seeing Kendall coming through the door. They let out a couple of squeals and rushed to him, hugging him as though he had risen from the dead. Susan took off running to get Rachael from the library, where she was attempting to get Beth down for a nap.

"Rachael, Kendall is back!" she screeched at the top of her voice.

Rachael's eyes grew big, and her mouth flew open. She stopped patting Beth and dashed out of the library, motioning for Susan to stay with the baby. Across the entrance hall and into the kitchen she flew. Wild horses wouldn't hold her back.

"Oh, thank you, God," she kept repeating as she hurried.

"I thought something terrible had happened to you, and I would never see you again," she wept, as she sailed into his arms.

She looked at his wonderful familiar face, and he drew her close, hugging her tightly.

"I'm okay—it's okay—I'm here," Kendall whispered close to her ear as he tried to comfort her. He gently kissed the tears on her cheeks.

Everyone was ecstatic that he had safely made his way home. Knowing how dangerous the streets outside the mansion were, it seemed a miracle that he had returned.

"Let's get the groceries in, and then I'll tell you all about my horrendous trip," he said, motioning to Paul and Martin to help him.

There was joy and laughter with each trip from the van to the kitchen, as the entire group gathered around. More wonderful than the sugar, rice, onions, and canned meats was the joy of having Kendall home safe.

As soon as the food was unloaded, Kendall couldn't keep the dramatics back as he told them about the two thugs who kidnaped him. Lillian and Connie listened but began making plans for a special dinner celebration. Special treats were the highlights of their life now, and this was an occasion to have one. Canned chicken with homemade cornmeal dressing was their choice. Dried potato flakes would make delicious whipped potatoes, dotted with lots of butter. Freshly baked biscuits, jellied cranberry sauce, and pineapple upside down cake for dessert would finish the meal perfectly. It would be a feast like Christmas all over again.

Kendall now home safe, Rachael's desire turned serious. She hoped that he would never leave her again. If she could hold on to him forever, she would do just that. Her heart wanted to be one with him every minute.

His trip created a traumatic separation which affirmed to both of them that they were not simply infatuated with one another, but truly in love. Rachael was ready to allow her deep affection for him to override any guilt about Grant. She would let go of the self-inflicted loyalty she felt toward him, and let go of the old tradition to wait at least a year. She sensed that Kendall's love was a gift given to her by God. It was as though heaven had reached into her life and blessed her in a special way, even in the turmoil surrounding every moment.

******

In the quiet of the night, after everyone had gone to bed, Rachael and Kendall stood near each other in the solarium. Rays of moonlight beamed down upon them while they talked and pledged their love to one another.

"Paul can marry us," Kendall said, making a note of the fact that he was a licensed minister. "It doesn't matter that we do not have a legal marriage certificate. In God's eyes we will be married, and that's all that matters."

Those were words that Rachael longed to hear. His commitment to her was like a shield of protection wrapping itself around every loss she felt, every heartache, and every worry. No longer would she have the burden of being the lone leader of the group, or a lonely widow marooned on a hill, afraid to wake up every morning. Kendall loved her, and together they would make a good team. His commitment to her meant that he was a faithful partner in the mission project. It would be his mission as much as it was hers.

The night was exceedingly beautiful, filled with romantic enchantment. Looking out through the solarium windows into the star-studded sky, every fear that she felt faded. The uncertainties she worked through each day would now be shared with Kendall. The fear of the mission being discovered by brutal authorities would be eased by his arms. Together they would struggle through the trenches and meet the challenges. Together they would carve out a new life, even in the midst of a world gone mad.

AT BREAKFAST THE NEXT MORNING, Kendall announced their engagement. Clicking a knife on his glass, he gained everyone's attention.

"I have something to announce, which gives me the most wonderful pleasure I have ever known. As you all know, Rachael and I are in love. Last night we affirmed our love and committed our lives to one another. I guess you would say we are engaged, and we want Paul to marry us."

Applause broke out around the table, along with a few loud hoots from Martin and Paul. There were hugs and a few happy tears from Maggie and Lillian.

Rachael was going to have happiness again. She would have the helpmate she needed and deserved. If her parents were here, they would give her their blessing and be proud of her. Grant would certainly approve of her sharing her love and her life and the mission with Kendall. *How beautiful it is,* she thought to herself, *that love can find a way when everything else is going wrong.*

******

Although there was no hall to rent, no wedding announcements to mail out, plans began immediately. The women embraced the role of directors and caterers, determined to make the wedding as beautiful and wonderful as possible.

It was a simple wedding, with everyone gathered in the grand room to witness the ceremony and enjoy the love and happiness that had come to Carson Hill. Lillian baked a three-tiered white cake and iced it with a creamy powdered sugar icing. Maggie gathered silk flowers from the vase in the entrance hall and tied them with a ribbon, making a beautiful bridal bouquet. Susan offered to take care of Beth so the couple could enjoy their wedding day.

Rachael selected a stunning pink chiffon gown from her wardrobe. The gown had been worn only once in New York City, at a formal function she and Grant attended less than two years ago. She shook off a self-inflicted feeling of guilt that tried to tone down her joy. *Grant and Daddy would approve of this marriage*, she convinced herself.

As radiant as any bride could possibly be, Rachael entered the grand room on the arm of Martin and then she took her place beside Kendall. Her beauty dazzled everyone, and Kendall found himself tingling from head to foot as he watched her enter the grand room.

"Will you take this man to be your wedded husband?"

The question came to her as if it were carried on the wings of a dove. The vows she pledged gave her love to Kendall for the rest of her life, whether long or short.

"I will."

Love is the will of the heart, and becoming one with Kendall would not solve all the problems they faced. Nor would the mad world stop and let them jump off. But marrying Kendall would melt her loneliness away and satisfy her intrinsic need for the love and devotion of a man.

******

Dawn came like the gentle brush of a feather across the face of a starry-eyed bride. While Kendall slept, Rachael slipped out of bed and into the chair to write in her journal.

> *February 15,*
>
> *My darling Kendall—You came to me when I was orphaned and widowed. Unsuspected and innocent, our lives intertwined and I again knew the thrill, yes the sheer absolute fun of being in love again. Though the world is in turmoil, my heart is alive and dancing in a beautiful spring-time of joy. In the despair of Grant's death, I was motivated by God to wait for what He desired to give to me. And while I waited I learned that "we must wait for God, long and meekly, in the wind and wet, in the thunder and lightning, in the cold and the dark, wait, and He will come [and give]. He never comes to those who do not wait."[1]*

******

For weeks, Esther's health had been under the watchful eye of Kendall. Her condition was weakening. The diuretics he was prescribing were not clearing the fluid from her lungs or her extremities. Her cardiovascular disease had progressed to serious cardiomyopathy, a terminal condition.

"I am going to double the diuretic you're taking with the hope it will keep the swelling down better," he told her, after examining her

---

1   Fr. Frederick William Faber, English hymn writer and theologian, 1814-1863.

carefully. "Continue to avoid salt at the table. It's difficult for you to avoid it entirely, considering the type of meals we have. With our shortages of fresh vegetables and meats, we are left with little alternative but to eat salty canned foods. But do what you can to avoid any extra. Move around the mansion as much as possible. The exercise will do you good." His care and instructions were appreciated, yet in Esther's mind there was no doubt what her body was telling her. She could no longer lie flat when sleeping.

"Thank you, Dr. Saunders," she said, "I'll do what I can, but I know this old body is failing."

A quick hug and pat on her shoulder and he was off to the kitchen. In the corner of the spice cabinet, Rose and Esther's medications were held safe and set up once a week in a seven-day pill holder.

"I am increasing Esther's diuretic," Kendall said to Connie, who passed the medications each morning to the two elderly ladies. "Please make sure that she gets two tablets at breakfast, rather than one."

Connie stopped wiping the counter and looked at him. "Is it serious?" she asked.

"Yes, I believe it is."

Silence fell between them. The funeral for Peter was only three months ago. Kendall thought how terrible it would be if another person died. This place was supposed to be a safe haven from death and destruction, yet it seemed like a war bunker, with survival promised only to the fittest. He was doing his best for Esther but it was not helping her failing heart. She was not going to get better, but he was keeping up a good front. Silently he was angry. He understood why Connie and some of the others often questioned why God allows evil? He had no answer. His questions were as deep and troubling as theirs. *If God is who He says He is, then why couldn't everything be perfect? Why do we have to contend with evil on a planet that God created in the first place?*

MARTIN NEVER FAILED TO HAVE the television news network turned on in the library during the day, except when Beth was napping. He was a news buff, but also just as afraid and jittery as the rest. Getting details of world conditions, and the latest news alerts, helped keep him and the others attuned to new global situations that might affect their private circumstances. Media warnings about new mayhem spreading in nearby cities gave the opportunity to plan survival strategies. It may not be a knock at the door that would chase them to the hiding place in the basement, but it might be swift military actions.

Every day reports of anarchy and videos of brutal officials taking people prisoner glared across the screen. The daily newspaper reports on the Internet told of whole sectors of societies disappearing. These ill-fated compatriots lived in the neighborhood precincts that were accused by the police of being insubordinate. Sometimes it was an entire ethnic group that was removed from their neighborhood.

Generation after generation of people had lived in these Detroit areas and birthed their babies there, raised the grandbabies, worked and played and lived in peace for decades. Their great-grandfathers and great-grandmothers survived the long and dangerous voyages from Europe to make their homes in this country. Their patriotism was beyond reproach. But it took only one or two renegades in these ethnic groups to create a situation that would bring in the authorities. Rather than seek out the defectors, the authorities found it easier to get rid of them all, especially if they were Jews. The tragic scenes of people being rounded up at gunpoint were comparable to the paranoia of Stalin and Hitler.

As late afternoon approached, residents prepared for bedtime and gathered in the dining room for dinner. The meal lacked sufficient protein but supplied plenty of long-lasting carbohydrates. Cream of chicken soup with chunks of canned tuna mixed in and served over large warm biscuits filled the plates and the hungry stomachs as well. Glasses of orange drink substituted for fruit. Small tulip-shaped dishes filled with rice pudding gave a hint of dessert, so sweet and so good. The children were still drinking reconstituted powdered milk, and the adults enjoyed hot tea.

Everyone settled in the grand room, with the lights again dimmed low and the drapes pulled tight across the large windows that faced Springfield Lake. Esther seemed anxious to talk about her deceased husband, Peter.

"Peter never talked about this," she began, "but I must tell his story before I die."

Everyone looked at her as if they were about to hear a joyful story full of adoration about Peter, but Esther's face was drawn and sad.

"In early 1945 Peter was herded onto a train with several thousand Jews being transferred from the Nazi Death Camp called Buchenwald. They were being taken to an unknown destination. The Nazis moved them because the allied forces were closing in, and they had to get rid of them. Peter was herded in with approximately one hundred-twenty-five others in a railroad car, as were several hundred more in the railroad cars that lined the tracks. These were boxcars with no ventilation and no sanitary provisions."

Martin wondered if the children should listen to this story, but curbed his uneasiness, thinking that many of the stories of the six million exterminated Jews during World War II had been lost, or silenced. So he didn't interrupt Esther. If the children understood what she was saying, they should stay and hear the story. Of course, it made it worse listening in dim light with the drapes drawn.

"They were squeezed in tighter than cattle, standing for several days as the train moved to an unknown place. Peter said the stench of feces and death was sickening. Suddenly bombs hit some of the boxcars. The train came to a crashing halt, and the doors on the car Peter was in flew open. Weak from hunger, he staggered out of the car, making his way over several fallen bodies.

"He was just a young boy, mysteriously escaping the Death Camp at Buchenwald because he was lucky enough that his number was not called for the gas ovens, but now he was a stranger in the Carpathian Mountains in Czechoslovakia. He hid in the forest to escape the German occupation.

"God helped him survive, leading him to a little village where he slept in the brush and woke one morning to find soldiers wearing green fatigues and helmets that had U.S. Army written on them. The allies had come. The war was over. The Americans gave him food.

"Why am I telling you this?" she said soberly. "I am telling you this because God does not abandon His people. He is not going to abandon us here at Carson Hill. We must trust that He has a plan for us. If we live or we die here on this hill, God will not forsake us. Peter came to believe that there is no death to a believer in the Messiah. Even though he sometimes longed for physical death in the terrible Death Camp at Buchenwald, where thousands starved to death before his eyes and dead bodies were wheel-barreled to the ovens by Jews half-dead themselves, he came to know life in Jesus Christ."

The group was challenged with these words. There was no story to follow this.

******

The unrest in the city was making bartering more and more difficult. Many trips were barren. The food supply was getting smaller, and meal planning was again getting extremely difficult for Lillian. Kendall was concerned about the nutritional needs of everyone. Spring in Michigan comes late on the calendar, generally around the middle of May. March was far too early to consider planting a garden to help supplement their food supply. Two months of lean, inadequate meals would take their toll on the two elderly women, and the children's growth as well. Kendall worried especially about his baby daughter, Beth. The powdered milk was the most important element of her diet. Should that run out, the baby would become malnourished.

Word on the Internet was buzzing that there was a good supply of fruit, meat, and grains coming to Michigan in trucks out of Florida. Hungry Chimera followers would flock to the Jackson Farmer's market and flood the area. Martin was scheduled to travel there in the morning. Hopes were high that the Florida delivery would arrive as scheduled because food from California was not reaching Michigan, or any of the eastern states, due to road destruction from the earthquakes. It would be months, possibly years, before major expressways were reconstructed. Planes were flying fruit and vegetables into Michigan, but the shipments were gobbled up by the giant supermarkets. Those who carried the mark of Chimera had no trouble getting food in the major grocery chains, but the defectors were suffering.

In search of reasonable prices as well as quantity, restaurant owners from as far away as northern Michigan and Wisconsin were leaving their areas to buy at the Jackson Farmer's Market. This could be a great plus for Martin, because the market place would be extremely crowded, and bartering less noticeable.

Rachael carefully sorted out several pieces of jewelry, a cameo locket, one pair of quarter carat diamond earrings, a diamond-studded gold pendant, and two of the gold watches. Martin would take all of this and hopefully come home with the van loaded from front to back. Hopes were high that he could easily get everything they needed, including powdered milk for baby Beth and the children.

A BLISTERY NORTHEAST WIND BLEW down from Canada, making the drive into Jackson cold and difficult. Heading into Jackson's downtown area, the van caught the wind and occasionally rocked back and forth. *Better to have wind than a blizzard*, Martin thought as he drove on the busy expressway.

As expected, numerous trucks and vans were already at the market place when he arrived. The place was swarming with restaurant chefs and proprietors crowding the premises, haggling to buy goods.

He found a place to park, but it was a long way off from the booths. He checked his pockets carefully, making sure the jewelry was safe. Before locking the van, he grabbed several huge shopping bags made of strong heavy cotton, each with wood handles sewn in tight to make carrying easier.

The wind was harsh, but the tall downtown buildings of Jackson helped to curb some of it. There were hundreds of people weathering the cold and mulling around the market grounds. Martin kept his eyes peeled for anyone who looked like a government agent. For sure, they would be here, watching for defectors. The ethnic dealers would be Martin's best bet to barter with. Many of them were extremely poor and usually looking for a generous deal. Some of them might be defectors and be selling their goods to get items for themselves to use for bartering. It was a crazy, mixed-up bag of likelihoods. He had to be very careful who he spoke to and what he said.

The sellers looked authentic, with their infrared scanners and computer registers, but they could also be camouflaged defectors of Chimera. No one working outside the system would tip their hand in a public place, so he would not know if he were bartering with a comrade or not.

Walking toward the booths, he spotted two Native American men selling smoked hams and dried beans. Behind the make-shift counter hung several Native American blankets. There were many buyers at this stand, picking over the hams. Quickly, Martin added up in his head that eight whole hams and fifteen pounds of beans would add up to approximately two hundred dollars in the Chimera system. The men would probably go for a watch, but the deal had to be made quickly. No one must see the transaction taking place.

He tossed four hams into one of the shopping bags. This was the way a buyer bought goods at the Jackson Market. They bagged them and then checked out at the cash register. He put four more in another bag, making sure the hams looked lean before taking them. In another bag he dropped fifteen one-pound bags of dried beans. He weighed himself down with poundage, but he must get these precious items regardless of the strain it took to carry them back to the van. He set the bags at the end of the counter, away from the pressing crowd, and waited to catch the eye of one of the booth operators.

It was several minutes before one of them finally noticed Martin standing there, waiting to pay for his goods. One of them left the small mob at the other end of the counter and approached him.

"Is this it?" the Native American said, looking into each bag.

"Yes," Martin answered and quickly flashed a watch.

The man looked at the watch and then quickly checked the crowd around the booth. No one was watching.

"I take back one ham and one bag of beans, and you take wool blanket instead, then you got deal," he said.

Martin didn't like him swapping back a ham and a bag of beans for a blanket that no one at the mansion needed, but the deal was laid out, and he had to take it. He shoved the watch in the man's hand and said, "Okay."

"You want help with those sacks?" the man asked.

There was no way he could carry the bags to the van unless he made another trip back to the counter, so he agreed to take help, knowing it was risky to let the man walk to the van. But his life was nothing but risks now anyway.

He unloaded the cloth bags after the man left and locked the van, going off to find another booth, again taking the cotton bags with him. He was cold from the sharp wind but thankful that he had bartered successfully for meat and beans.

The crowd was thickening and pressing even harder. While he hustled along the path in front of the booths, he could see only candies, clothing, and housewares. He needed to bring back flour and shortening, powdered milk, apples, and vegetables. The powdered milk was a must. He kept walking, looking for these items.

Making his way through the crowds, he watched for anyone who looked like a government agent. There were several uniformed police scattered here and there, and no doubt there were undercover agents swarming around looking for defectors trying to buy food without Chimera identification. He wouldn't know a secret agent if one looked him straight in the eye. He had to depend on God to keep him safe.

At last he spotted a booth with a variety of pastas and dried herbs and fresh vegetables. He shuffled his way through the crowd and up to the counter.

Glory be, he said to himself when he spotted boxes of dried milk. It was a strange item to be found in a farmer's market, but used by restaurant chefs to make creamy soups. Several vendors were manning this booth. There were hundreds of bags filled with pasta in all shapes and forms. There were dried tomatoes in cellophane packages and fresh parsley sprigs. Turnips with fresh green tops were piled next to big beautiful heads of white cabbage. Hanging vertically from the tarp behind the counter were hundreds of packages of gravy mixes, hooked together with clips. Next to the gravy mixes was a shelf filled with packages of powdered milk. He hit the jackpot at this booth.

He studied the goods for several moments, deciding how much he would buy and what pieces of jewelry he would offer. Before he was ready to deal, one of the vendors approached him and asked what he wanted to buy. He handed him several of the cloth bags.

"I'll take ten assorted packages of the pasta," he said, figuring that each of them weighed about two pounds.

"Also twenty gravy mixes, and all the powdered milk on the shelf," he said, pointing to them on the shelf behind the man.

The man put the items in the large cloth shopping bags.

"What else?" he asked.

"Five cabbages."

"Anything else?" the vendor asked.

"Yes, twenty packages of the dried tomatoes," he answered, motioning for him to drop them in the same bag as the cabbages.

While the vendor turned to get the dried tomatoes, Martin decided that the diamond-studded gold pendant would pay for the goods. When the vendor returned with the tomato packages, Martin checked to see if anyone was watching, before reaching into his pocket. To his left, he spotted a tall man watching him, as though he might be waiting his turn.

"Tell you what," he said to the vendor, "you wait on this man while I check to see if there is anything else I need." He didn't want to do business with someone standing so close. The man might be a secret cop.

The vendor diverted his attention away from him and onto the man who appeared to be waiting for his turn. Martin browsed around the booth, acting as though he might want to buy something else. The tall man left after buying pasta.

The vendor returned. Not saying a word, Martin flashed the diamond-studded pendant and waited for a response. The man said nothing.

"This is worth about fifteen hundred dollars," Martin quietly said to the vendor, who was taking a closer look. He leaned in closer to the vendor in an effort to hide his bartering transaction and looked around to see if anyone was watching. The horde of people at the end of the counter were busy purchasing foodstuff from the other vendors, and the crowd behind them was moving steadily along. No one appeared to be paying any attention to them.

The vendor looked closely at the pendant. He walked down to one of the other vendors and tapped him on the back. When he looked around, the man gestured for him to come over to where Martin was standing.

"This guy wants to pay for these things with this pendant," the vendor said to his partner. "He says it is worth fifteen hundred dollars."

Martin was getting nervous. These guys were taking far too long to close a deal.

The partner reached into this pocket and took out a small jeweler's magnifying glass. *Oh great,* he said to himself. *Now the guy has a magnifying glass. I'm going to be caught if they don't get on with this.* Obviously, Martin was not the first person these venders were accepting jewelry from. The man turned his back to the crowd and studied the pendant. Martin's heart was beating fast with fear. The few seconds the man took to examine the pendant seemed like an eternity. *Man, hurry up before someone sees you,* he thought to himself, as fear started mounting.

Finally the man turned around and nodded his head in approval. Martin let out the breath he was holding, gathered up the goods he bought, and lugged them back to the van, struggling with the weight, yet forging his way through the crowd as quickly as he could. *This would be enough for today,* he thought. *I can't push my luck.*

Downtown Jackson was like a busy beehive. The streets were congested with motorists who drove like they couldn't get to a fire fast enough. He wove his way through the traffic and onto the expressway, driving carefully so as not to draw attention or get into an accident. Behind his seat were the hams, dried beans, pasta, cabbages, dried tomatoes, and all the other good things he was successful in finding. Beth and the other children would have milk, and Lillian would be ecstatic.

In the rear-view mirror, he noticed a red Ford Taurus that had been steadily fixed behind him since he pulled out of the farmer's market place. It was now entering the expressway behind him. Was this simply someone traveling in the same direction as he, or was it a government agent following him?

He decided to exit off a ramp before his normal turn, hoping to lose the Taurus. To his disappointment it kept pace with him, turning whenever he turned. While stopped at a traffic light, he saw in the mirror that the driver was a woman dressed in garb that resembled a uniform. At the neckline of her jacket was a white blouse buttoned at the collar with a short, double knotted navy-blue tie. There was no doubt that she was a government agent and that she was following the van. She must have spotted him bartering for food, and probably ran a check on the license plate and found it to be bogus. He reached for the cell phone and called the mansion. Kendall answered.

"Kendall, I'm on my way back, and I've got what appears to be a government agent following me," he said with concern.

He went on while Kendall listened, "I'm going to abort my direction and drive to Summerset. I'll try to lose her on those back roads. I won't come back until I know I've lost her. This may take some time."

"Take care, brother, and be careful," Kendall cautioned. "We heard there are roadblocks on US 25 near Centerville, so stay clear of that area."

"Roger," Martin answered, and ended the conversation.

Turning left toward Summerset, he increased his speed and swerved onto a dirt road, making the turn on two wheels, and then barreling off the road into a tall thicket of dormant bushes. The road forked at the turn. *What a break,* he said to himself. One fork led north to Hillsdale, the other south to Jonesville. He quickly turned off his engine and sat quietly, hidden in the brush. The red Taurus zoomed by, heading straight toward Hillsdale.

His heart beating furiously, he sat quietly, hoping the woman in the red Taurus would not return and discover the van sitting in the underbrush. A few minutes passed. He could hear a car coming back up the road. Sure enough, it was the red Taurus, flying like a bat out of hades. He held his breath and saw the car turn onto the main highway without spotting him. *Oh, thank You, Jesus!* he said to himself. After a few minutes longer to make sure the woman was gone, he pulled out.

Arriving back in the Irish Hills, he parked in one of the four garages adjacent to the kitchen entrance. He quickly pushed the button and closed the door behind him. The van and the food now safely tucked into the garage, he ran toward the kitchen door. Kendall was watching him run toward the mansion and quickly disarmed the security and held the kitchen door open.

"Did you lose the car?" Kendall blurted out as Martin ran through the door.

"I'm pretty sure I did," he said, storming inside and taking off his jacket. He ran fingers through his hair as if to straighten himself up.

"I'll tell you, man," he continued, "It wasn't easy today. I guess I should be thankful only one demon was after me because I'm sure Jackson was crawling with police."

Rachael and Lillian walked into the kitchen, wanting to know about his escape from the government agent, and what he was able to bring back. He reached deep into his pockets and brought out the earrings and the watch that he did not use and handed them back to Rachael.

"Does this mean you did not bring much back?" There was disappointment in her voice.

"On the contrary," he answered enthusiastically. "I have smoked hams, dried beans, cabbages, pasta, dried tomatoes, fresh turnips greens, and powdered milk, lots of good things."

"Wonderful!" Lillian howled and threw her arms around him.

******

At dusk, Kendall walked outside and across the edge of the property, looking down at the road below for any sign that the mansion was being watched. A few cars passed, and lights were burning in some of the homes along the lakeshore, but there was no sign that the mansion was under surveillance. As soon as it was completely dark, the men unlocked the garage and brought in the food.

It was a long day. Martin was exhausted. Bedtime came early for him.

Rachael tucked Beth snugly into her crib, kissed Kendall, and set her flashlight at an angle on the small writing desk, to make an entry in her journal.

March 13. Once again our coffers are full and God has protected us. Though this night seems tranquil, I am reminded that our struggle is not against flesh and blood, but against the evils of darkness in this fallen world. And I know full well that there is no victory without war, and no happiness without pursuit and no purpose without true commitment. Although I curse the evil that has ruined my world and brought hardship, still I know that I, like everyone in this mansion, need more than physical ease.

A goldfish has that. We need more than the will to live. More than a warm bed and a full stomach. We need purpose, and with that a strong commitment to ourselves and one another to stay resolved to continue to obey God's commands and never give in to Chimera. We need to trust you Lord, for even more than you gave today.

CHAPTER 10
THE PREACHER

"IF WE DIDN'T NEED TO eat, we would be fine," Connie said as she helped Lillian gather food items for dinner. Some items were getting low again, and if that was not enough to worry about, the authorities were clamping down harder. It was unsafe to walk anywhere without Chimera ID. People suspected of taking items from someone in a public place for payment of goods were immediately imprisoned, or shot on the spot. The authorities were not standing down on any hint of insubordination. Paul tried to barter in Lansing, but security guards and police officers were swarming the market places in unheard-of numbers. Independent grocery stores had full-time officers watching. There was a madness in the air. It was plain insanity, and again Esther was reminded of what it was like in Europe during World War II.

"I am a Jew!" she blurted out, looking rather upset at the group sitting in the grand room, all of whom were engaged in conversation after eating a very lean lunch. They stopped talking and looked at her.

"During World War II, my descendants were hunted like animals in Europe," she said, ready to give another lesson on the horrors of war. "You and I, dear friends, are like the Jews seventy-five years ago. We are hungry, and we are hunted because we belong to God."

After saying that, she wept bitterly, longing for her dead husband, who was not there to comfort her. Her words penetrated deep into everyone's heart. She was right; they were just like her husband Peter, when he was escaping the Germans during World War II, like the scattered Jews, who were hunted down by the authorities and killed, or starved, or tortured to death. Their situation seemed no different. Except that Jew or gentile, no matter what race or creed, if you were not using the worldwide system, you were predestined to die, either by the hands of evil government agents or lack of food.

EVERY MAJOR CITY THROUGHOUT THE US, and the entire world for that matter, was being policed as though a dictator was in control. The worldwide computer system had taken away every individual's worth under the false guise of equality. Rachael looked around the room, noticing how everyone had lost weight. As much as possible, the children were given their regular portions, but the adults were often going without. It was almost too much for her to bear. The planting season was six weeks away, depending on an early spring. Even if they could hold out, where would vegetable seeds come from, and how long would it take them to germinate and grow? Lillian had saved seeds from a few tomatoes they had weeks ago. The potatoes that remained when planting season arrived could be cut and planted, but they were hardly enough to survive on.

Of all the residents, Connie was the most embittered and outspoken. She could not understand why God would allow this to happen. She could not come to grips with His promises in comparison with their suffering. She was also having trouble believing that Christians are supposed to act perfect, as if they never sin.

"We are just as nuts and illogical as The Great Ten Nations," she blurted out. "We are Christians who are trying to do good, but for what? Who are we fooling? Look at us, we are stuck in this place, trying to trust God and survive while everything around us is crumbling. I just don't get it. And don't ask me to be perfect! I'm not, and I can't be!"

It was like everything that bothered her had suddenly exploded. A dead silence fell over the room, while everyone waited for the other person to answer. Was there an answer, and if so, who had it? If her questions could not be answered, then was there something that could be said to bring her peace?

Paul got up and walked to the large thick hassock in the middle of the room and sat down. He cleared his throat and began to speak to all of them, but mainly he eyed Connie.

"Someone years ago made a statement that stuck to my brain like a ball of gummy dumplings thrown at a wall," he began. "It went something like this: Christians are the most illogical people in the world. They spend their entire lives striving for what they will never become.

"I had to agree," he went on. "All I needed to do was look at my life. I was living the most illogical existence a person could drum up. I was getting up every morning with the expectations that I could pass through the day without saying or doing anything that resembled sin, and whatever happened I had to accept without any qualms. I thought all Christians lived above sin. Of course, I never attained this pinnacle of perfection, so to ease the agony of my defeat, I often redefined my sin as weakness."

He glanced around the room and then directed his next statement to Connie.

"The statement that Christians are illogical is correct. The Bible tells the Christian that they are transformed into new creatures once they believe in Christ, everything supposedly changes for them and they are no longer slaves to sin. Yet a few pages from that, the Apostle Paul complains about how he is always doing what he shouldn't be doing, and not doing the things he should do. He's in a terrible fix. There's a war going on inside him. Finally, in emotional exhaustion he blurts out, 'Oh wretched man that I am who will deliver me?' Then he answers his own question by saying, Christ."

No one interrupted. Paul had every eye and every ear, and no one knew where he was going with this. There was much intrigue hanging in the air.

"Well, what the Apostle Paul said was true," he continued. "Christ no doubt was delivering him, but when and where was the deliverance? Is God's intervention at the Genesis or at the Revelation?"

His eyes swept completely around the room and steadied again on Connie.

"The statement that Christians are illogical stirred up thoughts and I found myself considering that I continuously struggled for perfection that I would never achieve. Reality convinced me that I was without a doubt, totally illogical when thinking that I would be perfect on this earth and that anyone or anything would be perfect."

He stood up and walked to the fireplace and turned around to face the group.

"In serious deliberation with this dilemma—which started nagging at me in the prime of my Christian experience—I tore myself back to the beginning chapters of the Bible—you know, that part where God created Adam and Eve and gave them instructions that they were not to eat the fruit from a certain tree.

"The serpent coaxed Eve into eating the fruit against God's command, and she, in turn, gave the fruit to her husband. Thus, the whole world was immediately ruined by two people's disobedience."

By this time Connie was getting confused. *What is this man driving at,* she asked herself?

Paul continued, "I had hoped to rediscover some sort of hidden 'gold' in the beginning story of man's creation. I wanted the answer to my question about logic and why Adam and Eve could not resist the serpent, but I found no answer. At least not in black and white. The story in Genesis left me with the concept that the serpent really pulled a good one over on Adam and Eve."

He looked around the room and noticed that everyone was listening, except Esther who had fallen asleep and Susan who was yawning. But he kept going.

"So, where is the logic in the beginning of creation? I mean, why would a fallen angel like Satan be allowed to con God's precious creation into disobedience, and consequently ruin things for everyone? Yes, I do mean ruin everything, because after Satan beguiled Adam and Eve, beasts got wild, thorns grew, weeds came, insects started stinging, storms came up, pestilence persisted, women had to bear their children in pain, men had to work by the sweat of his brow, and everything eventually died."

At that, he walked back to the hassock and sat down, while everyone stayed silent, waiting for his point.

"Pretty grim start to such a wonderful thing, wouldn't you say? Look at it this way: a chef in his kitchen decides to make a cake. So he gathers the ingredients and mixes up a luscious cake batter. He pours the batter into baking pans and then carefully places it into an oven that has been heated to just the right temperature. When it is baked and cooled, he places it on a beautiful serving plate and puts a delicious frosting on it. His creation is now completed, so he sets it on the table and says, 'this is really a good thing that I have created.' He then stands back and allows someone to enter the kitchen and destroy the cake, even though he could stop them if he wanted to. Make any sense? Hardly. And so in many respects the story of Eve and Satan doesn't make sense to the analytical mind either."

No one dared interrupt him, although there was concern about his words. It appeared that he was bashing his own religious ideology. How could he do this and comfort Connie?

He went on, "Here's another thought, our battles never stop. Whether we are here fighting to avoid Chimera or we are isolated on an island somewhere in the south pacific, the battle between good and evil goes on. I remember something I read a while back, written by John Barber, in Impact. It was titled 'Holding Back the Flood', or something like that. Barber put it this way: because man disobeyed God, He placed a curse upon man and the earth, including living creatures, plants, and insects. Everything God created was put on a downhill slope to death. It is, therefore, not possible to preserve the creation as it was in its original state, only possible to conserve it. So, in laypersons language, it is not possible to eliminate sin.[2]

"So I ask this question: why didn't God curtail Satan, rather than allowing all of us to be born with sinful natures? Why couldn't we

2   John Barber, Holding Back the Flood, *Impact*, September 2002, Coral Ridge Ministries, Fort Lauderdale, FL.

have been born learning how to be bad, rather than needing to be taught how to be good?"

He stopped for a moment and pointed to Beth, who was sleeping on Kendall's lap.

"Have you ever seen a baby that was born knowing how to be perfectly good? No, a baby automatically knows how to be bad. As wonderful as Beth is, she is being taught how to be good. Her nature knows how to be bad. So, why do we fight what we can't stop? Why are we so illogical?"

He looked around, wondering if anyone would care to stab at an answer, but no one wanted to speak. He was deliberately playing it coy, being obnoxiously puzzling on purpose. He was pulling them in like fish caught in a net.

"Look at it this way," he continued, "every born again Believer trusts in a God they have never seen, and in a Savior they have never touched. They believe in heaven, though they have never personally talked to anyone who has been there. They believe in the resurrection of the body, though they have not seen anyone raised from the dead. Yes, we Christians are about as illogical as they come. So I needed an answer to what almost seemed insaneness. There I was, bent on pleasing a God I had never seen, and expecting God to make everything perfect."

He looked straight at Connie when he said that.

"Here's the kicker, my own personal saneness came in a simple answer. I could be no other way than the way I was, because we all are bound, or strapped, in *perfect order within an environment of both good and evil.* Perfect order illustrates to us that earth is ninety-nine million miles away from the sun. It tilts exactly twenty-three degrees in order to give us four seasons. The moon gives us two ocean tides a day and keeps the planet from flooding. When these statistics are thoroughly examined, it seems convincing that such *perfect order* could be masterminded only by someone Divine.

"A fallen world was not the way God desired it to be, but man's disobedience caused it. Understand this, God wanted his human creation to love him. He didn't want robots forced to love and forced to obey. So by giving us free will choice, this would give God love out of free will from the person he created.

"Now, back to the garden and Eve chomping away at that apple. She was told by her Creator not to eat that fruit. This was God's way of giving her a choice, an avenue in which she, as an absolutely free-willed human being, could say I love you and trust you. In other words, I'll obey you and not eat this apple, because you are my Creator and you have told me not to do this, and I love you enough to not eat this apple. Or she could say, I don't love you and I don't trust you, and I'll do what I want. The choice was given. Then entered Satan, whom God allowed to tempt her and test her allegiance. We know the result.

"Eve was created for love and obedience. You and I are created for love and obedience, too, otherwise we would be robots to God."

Connie slid forward to the edge of her chair and said, "I follow what you have been saying, but I still don't understand why we all have to suffer the consequences of Eve's disobedience?"

She was getting down to brass tacks by asking the question that most people ask when they try to figure out the universe and the Almighty. Was there an answer?

Paul walked to the fireplace again and turned and faced everyone, but again, directed his comments to Connie.

"Although we might think that it is totally illogical for us to suffer on this earth when we cannot see the good in it, or to trust in a God and a Savior we have never seen or touched, or strive for perfection that can never be reached, the truth is that the mystery of God and his trustworthiness is in the midst of all that we question. For you see, God is not set with boundaries or beginnings or ends like we are, nor is he required to explain His reasoning. He is neither logic nor illogic, but he is in the realm of Spirit. He manifests himself to us with His Spirit to our spirit. Someday, we will understand all things. When you and I personally experience eternal life after death, that will be the absolute reality for us. Until then, there are no absolutes on Carson Hill. When we see the Lord and know Him as he is, then there will be perfect answers and absolutes. Until then things may appear illogical, even insane. Eternal life, Connie, is the *absolute we look for, and our victory.*"

The moment in which each of them was living called for a keen cognizant faith, a faith that was acute and conscious. Each individual had come to the mansion because of their common belief that evil was driving the nations. Each had come because they were in need and because they feared for their safety. They believed that the world's new financial system would soon expand to take control of every individual's life, as well as their financial wealth. They were there because they belonged to God, not the government. They were there because Rachael had been coached by God's Spirit for this very moment in time, when a handful of believers in Christ would find refuge in her mansion. Day after day, in the little things that transpired between them, it was the experience of their love for each other and the hope they had in their hearts that bolstered their faith. Paul was right. There were no absolutes on Carson Hill, but the meaning of life could be found in their testimony, though never seeing God, still they knew Him through His powerful Spirit.

BEFORE SHE WOULD ALLOW HERSELF to fall asleep, Rachael opened her journal and took her pen in hand and wrote:

> *April 9. To the dark unbelieving heart, you, God, are the smell of death, but to those who will be saved, you are the fragrance of life. Who can equal that? Unlike the hungry millions who float in tureens of false persuasions, my life takes its' meaning in You alone. I have given all to you, and with no regret. Yet, in return, you have given me everything. And so I give thanks. I ask that You give Connie peace and understanding.*

******

Kendall made a risky trip to the Eastern Market in Detroit, knowing that the danger of getting caught bartering would land him in jail, or get him killed. Still, he had to try for the sake of everyone at the mansion, especially the children. He left early enough to be on the expressway in the middle of the morning rush hour. In many respects these trips were getting to be old hat because they were so frequent. But there was nothing old hat about the danger. Arriving at the market place he carefully scouted for those vendors that appeared to be poor and would be most likely to take the gold items he offered.

Police were watching people closely. One careless move and he would never return. He parked the van and walked to the busiest section of the market place, mingling in close with the crush of people.

As providence would have it, he found two Arab vendors that would barter. Between these two posts Kendall got plenty of powdered milk and eggs, plus two ten pound wooden boxes of mild cheese and three twenty-pound bags of self-rising flour. This was the easiest trip he made. Pulling out of the parking area, a cop waved him on with hardly a glance.

******

It was midday, April 14, and the air outside was warm. Maggie opened small windows throughout the mansion, allowing fresh country air to enter. Spring was coming early to Michigan with temperatures hitting record highs. Martin and Paul prepared a sunny clearing in the woods for a large vegetable garden. Seeds from every vegetable they were fortunate to buy from the market vendors had been carefully dried and stored for planting.

Maggie went on with her work, gathering the dirty bed linens into the first-floor laundry room. Suddenly she caught sight through the small window above the washer of several men with dogs on leashes lurking around the side of the mansion. She dropped what she was doing and rushed to the library, where Kendall and Paul were watching news reports.

"They're here!" she cried, running as fast as she could get to them. "They're outside with dogs and guns."

Immediately Kendall ran for Rachael, who was in the grand room playing with Beth and Duke. Esther and Rose were also there, reading in a quiet corner.

"Get to the cellar!" he yelled as he neared them. "There are police and dogs outside!"

Just then, the pounding began on the doors, both front and back. Lillian and Connie were startled in the kitchen. They ran from the kitchen, terrified to find Martin gathering the children with the help of Laura and Karen. Frantically, Esther and Rose hurried out of the grand room, following Rachael. Everyone was in the cellar hideout in a flash.

The loud pounding at the doors didn't let up until the side kitchen door was broken and the alarm sirens started blasting.

The camouflaged door on the cellar was tightly closed after Rachael accounted for everyone. The lights were turned on, and Kendall motioned for everyone to stay quiet. The children were frightened and shaking, but they stayed mute.

The group had gone through several practice drills, but the real thing was much different than anyone expected. Heavy breathing slowed down while each mother wrapped their arms around their children, encouraging them not to cry or make a sound. Rose sat with both arms around Esther, comforting her while she gasped for air. The run to the basement was almost more than her weak heart could take. Kendall quickly rummaged through the medical supplies and found the nitro and shoved one of the small pills under Esther's tongue. The security alarm could be heard faintly through the walls of the cubby. The alarms would stop and reset in ten minutes, then stop entirely.

Rachael knew there would be clues the intruders would see, tipping them off that there were people hiding. The smell of lunch was still in the air. The kitchen still had dirty dishes on the counters. The piles of dirty laundry in the laundry room was a dead giveaway that there were several people living in this mansion.

The dogs sniffed throughout the first floor, while the armed police opened and slammed doors and cupboards. When no one was found, the upstairs was searched. Human scents were all over the mansion, in every room. The dogs were in an excited frenzy.

Guns still drawn, they moved to the basement. The dogs picked up human scents on the cement floor and tracked them to the wall of the hidden cubby. Behind the wall hearts were pounding uncontrollably, while the sound of toenails scratching and barking terrorized them more. The mothers held their children tight and whispered to them not to make a sound. Beth was given a pacifier to keep her from crying. The men positioned themselves along the inside wall of the cubby so if the police started shooting, the bullets would hit them and not the women and children.

The dogs stayed focused on one spot, scratching at the camouflaged door. Examining it closely, the police determined that the place the dogs were scratching and barking at must be a hidden door.

"They're in here all right," one of the cops said. "Go get a crowbar from the squad car." He motioned for one of them to get it while he kept feeling along the wall.

With clubs and a crowbar, they began beating upon the wall near the concealed entrance. The sound was terrifying. The children were now crying and screaming with fear. There was nothing anyone could do but keep breathing words like, "save us Lord."

As soon as Martin saw a police officer through the torn wall, he called out.

"Don't shoot, we'll come out peacefully!"

One by one, they stepped through the ripped doorway and surrendered to the authorities.

Rachael's effort to save her home and save these poor victims crumbled in just a moment of time. Everything that took place in the last several months flashed through her mind, like someone taking their last breath. The police assembled the group in the grand room, where an interrogation was conducted. Rachael disclosed only what was obvious but did not give any details. The others gave their names and answered the questions asked of them. For now, there was no force or brutality used. The children hung on their mothers. Esther stumbled to a chair and literally fell into it, crying, "Please don't hurt us, please don't take the children."

One of the officers working outside came into the mansion and disclosed that there were two vans in the garage.

"The stables are empty," he said. "We found a gas tank and also a huge generator. Looks like these people are planning to hold up for quite some time."

The head officer rummaged through the desk in the library, hoping to find important documents, but he found only the nonsensical papers Rachael had deliberately placed in the desk to throw authorities off.

"Where are the keys to the vans?" the head officer asked.

"In the cutlery drawer in the kitchen," Rachael answered.

The officer motioned for one of his subordinates to get the keys.

"You there," the officer said, pointing to Martin, "you're going to drive one of the vans."

"What! Where are we going?" Martin asked, his face white with fear.

"Never mind, you just do what you're told," the answer came back.

"You," he continued, pointing to Kendall. "You're going to drive the other van."

The vans were pulled around to the front of the mansion. At gunpoint, everyone was ordered to get in and take a seat. Laura and her children got into the van Martin was to drive. Following her was Maggie, Lillian, Connie, and Connie's son, Nathan. Rachael took a seat in the van Kendall was to drive, followed by Karen, Paul, and their children, along with Esther and Rose.

Martin and Kendall were then instructed to follow the police car leading the way. Behind the two vans would be another police vehicle, keeping them sandwiched in. A police officer and a canine boarded each van. Everyone was instructed to keep their mouths shut and stay seated.

Rachael held Beth close, wondering where they were being taken. She looked toward the mansion and saw Duke. *Everything is gone,* she said to herself, *including Duke. He will starve to death.* As they pulled away from the mansion, her heart sank into despair. Her mission was over. Tears filled her eyes, and she buried her face in Beth's blanket and muffled her pitiful crying.

It was not the fear of death that frightened them, as much as it was the awareness of evil. Literally, it could be felt pouring out on them from the police, as though they had no conscience, no sense of right and wrong. The world was in the throes of delusion and penetrating satanic evil.

The vans pulled out and down the hill. Esther was bundled up in a heavy down-filled jacket that was left in the van from one of the bartering trips. She wiped the tears from her eyes on the sleeve while she caught her last glimpse of the Irish Hills mansion. Rose sat motionless while the children leaned upon their mothers. Sorrow and fear were making its bed in everyone's heart. Kismet's appointment had come unexpectedly. Where would it end? Where was God?

Rachael watched Kendall's face in the rear-view mirror as they headed east toward Detroit. Every so often, he glanced into the mirror and saw her staring at him. Their eyes silently asking, *where are we going and what will happen.* The caravan continued east, along M-50, toward Detroit.

CHAPTER 11

THE SIEGE

THE HEAD POLICE CAR TURNED, leading the caravan southeast on Southfield Road into the city of Ecorse, an established suburban community closely tied to Detroit's southwest side. Rachael noticed the various storefronts along the route. She recognized some of the chain stores, all belonging now to the government. The metro area was very much alive despite the oppression. Parking lots at the strip malls were surprisingly full, and stores appeared to maintain active patrons. Even if they could escape from the vans, no one would risk rescuing them.

Driving further on Southfield Road, they neared Biddle Avenue, adjacent to the Detroit River. People on the street were gawking at the caravan, actually stopping to look. The police cars and vans slowly inched their way to the edge of the river waterfront. Inching up to the shoreline, the lead car stopped, and the head officer got out. Although there were fishing boats and barges docked along the shoreline, the place was otherwise deserted. The appearance gave evidence that there had been no fishing at this particular spot for quite some time. Stranger still, it appeared that the boats had been abandoned. Kendall took note that a large Wayne County Sheriff boat was tied securely to what resembled a new dock. With that observance, it dawned on him that the lead officer was the newly appointed County Sheriff, and the other officers were deputies. Elections had stopped when the coalition of The Great Ten Nations emerged on the world scene, taking over all city and government detail. These men were simply appointed officers, wearing a badge.

Although the mission group would technically be considered citizens of the county they resided in, jurisdiction laws under the new world order were abandoned. Arrests and confiscations were made by any government-appointed officer. It appeared to Kendall that these officers were enjoying their appointed roles and ready to do harm to them in whatever way pleased them.

The head officer, now identified as a sheriff, told everyone to get out and stand along the sides of the vans. Esther struggled to climb out, her feeble legs hardly able to hold her. Maggie rushed to her aid and took hold of her arm, gently helping her out.

The sight of the Irish Hill's family lined up against the vans played a scene in Esther's memory from photos taken decades ago, when the Germans lined up hundreds of Jews at the edge of a huge pit. They humiliated them by making them strip off their clothes, and then blasted machine gun bullets into their naked bodies. Most of them fell into the pit, some dead, some still alive. Bulldozers revved up their engines and shoved the dirt back into the hole, catching the bodies of those who fell on the edge and tumbling them into the pit along with the dirt. The Nazis buried them without mercy or respect. It was a scene Esther thought was seared from her memory, but there it was, holding on like a stubborn mule that would not relent, surfacing to the front of her mind with this caustic action by the these malicious police.

She remembered the year of 1939, when her happiness as a Jew in Poland was suddenly turned into fear. Adolph Hitler was eager to wipe out the "vermin" of Europe. She was fifteen years old that year when the Nazis smashed down the front door of her home and carried her parents off, along with her and her sisters, separating them from each other and sending them to separate concentration camps. She never saw her family again. Arriving in America some years later, she felt safe. Nothing like this would ever happen again, not in America.

As far as the world was concerned, she knew that the shadows of Hitler's atrocities could never be fully described. Many in the world chose to deny what happened, but she was one of Hitler's victims. She personally witnessed the horrors in the camps where she was held.

Somehow this scene at the Detroit waterfront could be the same fate, she thought. Her husband, Peter, was sent to Buchenwald, where the nauseating stench of burning human flesh permeated the air. The crematoriums operated twenty-four hours a day. Could the residents of Carson Hill be going to their cremation? Her mind went back again to Peter. She remembered he waited during days filled with fear and nights filled with despair for his number to be called. Those waiting back then had the same fear that hovered over Carson Hill. Esther recalled how he wept as he told her of the cries of men and women and boys and girls.

As providence would have it, the allied forces were closing in, and Peter escaped. But who would rescue the residents of Carson Hill, here in this deserted area of the Detroit River? How different their scene was from Peter's. It was cold when he survived the Nazis. It was warm here, but the same fear was present. *How fortunate,* she thought as memories and thoughts raced through her mind, *that his rescue by* the U.S. Army and merciful MP's led him eventually to America, to find her. Her thoughts continued to reel, *I will count it a privilege to die for what I believe in. Yes, even more of an honor to die because I am a Christian Jew.*

The children were terrified of the police, but oddly enough, none of them were crying. Each family huddled close together. The single women and Nathan clung to each other. Kendall made his way up the line, looking at each one as he walked passed them. He was far too angry to be afraid.

"We are American citizens, and you have no right to be taking us away from our home," he said to the officers.

The sheriff walked up to him and gave him a shove into the side of the van and said, "You are traitors. You are insubordinate."

Kendall bounced back off the side of the van, yelling, "We are Americans who merely want to protect our independence and what we and our fathers have worked for. You have no right to be doing this, and I demand that you release us and let us go back to our home."

His words infuriated the officers.

The thug-like officials were wholly allied with The Great Ten Nations. The world-wide scheme was hallowed doctrine to them. Their consciences were seared, and they would not tolerate anyone being insubordinate.

The sheriff walked over to him, drew his fist tight, and punched him in the stomach, with a blow so hard that he doubled over in pain and fell to the ground.

"How dare you!" Rachael cried as she quickly set Beth down on the ground and worked to help Kendall up.

Lillian, fighting the immense adrenalin that was racing through her body, and desperately trying to steady her knees that were ready to buckle, picked Beth up and leaned against the van in an effort to stay standing upright.

Martin and Paul stepped forward and in front of Kendall to protect him. The sheriff would have to go through them to get at him again. While the commotion went on, the other officers looked on in amusement, smirking and laughing as though they loved human fear and suffering.

The rapidly deteriorating state of affairs was more than convincing. The enemy of man's soul was powerful, and standing directly in front of them, to mock and blaspheme God. Although the group had listened for several months to reports of brutality worldwide, they were now experiencing it firsthand.

"When the Commissioner finds out that we secretly pulled these defectors out of Lenawee County, he is going to give us the Congressional Medal of Honor for sure," one of them said, laughing hardily.

"Yeah, we sure scooped the local patsies on this one," another officer laughed.

The round-up of innocent citizens by thugs wearing a police badge was like wild animals hunting innocent prey, with a prize for the one who could find and destroy the most. Kendall was sickened as he thought of how brutal and callous these men were, yet at the same time, he realized from their conversations that only these four officers were aware of the mission in the Irish Hills. If they could escape, they could go back without worry. These guys had come in secret, to steal the thunder of the local police and to steal whatever they could from the mansion. If the group could manage to get away, they would remain free. But with guns waving at them, they were helpless.

The sheriff straightened his pants around his fat stomach and told them to form a line and start walking to the sheriff's boat. He pointed to the large half-roofed cruiser with the emblem on the side. They obeyed and moved away from the vans, boarding the boat like cattle going to the slaughterhouse. While everyone crowded into the boat and sat on the bench seats, an officer started the engine. It sputtered and bubbled, intensifying the horrifying fear of uncertainty everyone felt. Fearful questions were in all their minds. Where were they going? What would be done to them?

Susan began screaming with terror as the boat pulled away from the shoreline. The moment gave the impression that she had suddenly realized they were going to die. Her shrieking started the other children crying, and immediately each mother held their child and spoke comforting words that seemed almost as useless as telling them everything was okay.

"Shut those kids up!" one of the officers yelled, waving his gun at them.

Paul got up and touched each child, telling them to stop crying. "Remember all you have learned at the mansion. Don't be afraid."

The forced excursion had taken five long hours, and now the night air was moving in, and it was getting cold. Everyone was shivering, even Esther, who was still wearing the jacket left in the van. The boat cruised steadily east. Paul quickly got his bearings and realized where they were heading. He leaned toward Martin and Kendall and whispered. "I think they're taking us to Mud Island."

The thought of Mud Island escalated their fears. Local television stations had carried reports of mass killings on this small island, located in the middle of the Detroit River channel. The island was one of many places the authorities chose to execute those they claimed were insubordinate to the new world order. This was a madness that was only heard of in third world countries. How could such a horrible thing come to America? Mud Island was the place where entire neighborhoods were brought when defectors were found among them. Execution became the fastest way of getting rid of Christian rebels because the jails were overflowing. Shallow graves were dug, and some bodies were burned when the wind would carry the stench away from Detroit. This was a nightmare, like a horror movie coming to life.

Maggie began to pray softly under her breath as the boat kept pushing eastward through the choppy waters. There was nothing else they could do but pray and hope that God would somehow find a way to deliver them from the hands of these brutal officers. Her low voice carried through the boat, bringing an immediate response from the sheriff. He got up and walked toward her, moving in a staggering zigzag fashion as the boat veered and cut through the waves. Placing his left hand on the back of the bench in front of Maggie, to steady himself, he swung his right hand, slapping her face hard.

"Stop that, you disgusting wretch!" he yelled at her.

At that, Paul immediately jumped to his feet and took hold of the sheriff, but he was shoved off, with a gun pointed in his face.

"Sit down, scum," the sheriff yelled.

Everyone gasped at what just happened. Connie quickly slid her arm around Maggie's shoulder, trying to ease the situation, knowing that the slap was still stinging.

"I'm okay," she said, glaring at the sheriff.

The second deputy hurried to the back of the boat, curious about the commotion.

"We got us a Sunday school group here on this boat," the sheriff told him in a sarcastic and irreverent tone. "This guy, here, wants to protect the lady," he said, pointing to Paul.

"I do believe that these are holy-rollers," he laughed. "They're the worst kind, you know."

The sheriff pointed his gun again at Paul. Susan started crying uncontrollably again, with her face buried in her hands so she wouldn't see her father shot.

"Get up to the front of the boat," he ordered Paul. "And you there, the great American," he said, pointing the gun at Kendall, "You get up there with him."

The boat surged toward Mud Island through the rough cold waters. When they reached Mud Island, it was almost dark. A full moon helped to light the shoreline, which was mucky and covered with wild reeds and small rocks. A new dock had been erected for the sheriff's boat, and it clearly testified that boats were coming to this island and atrocities were on-going here.

Without anyone speaking a word, the boat was docked, and they disembarked at the silent directive of a waving pistol that motioned them ashore.

"Form a line and walk behind me," the sheriff ordered.

He turned, and with a bright-beamed flashlight shining upon a well-beaten path, he started walking, and they followed. The three deputies walked at the rear of the group, each of them holding a flashlight. The path led into a thickly wooded area several yards offshore. Esther was lifted by both Maggie and Lillian in order to keep up. Karen helped Rose, who was prone to stumbling because of poor night vision and arthritic ankles. Rachael held Beth tight, while at the same time allowing

Michael to hold onto her arm. The other children walked single file, behind Laura. Their fathers were up ahead, following the lead officer, as commanded.

This scene seemed ironic and pitiful to Rachael. *We are helping each other to our death,* she thought to herself. *The wealth of my parents, the encouragement of Grandpa Carson, the plan that Grant and I put together, all of it will be lost if we can't do something quick,* she thought. *My faithfulness to God and my allegiance—what good is it now? My plans have brought these people to this deserted place, where all our hopes and dreams for the future will be buried with our dead bodies.*

Her thoughts were agonizing, as she tried to exercise a measure of faith that would allow God to work. She believed in miracles, but would God give them one? The wind blew across the island, carrying the stench of rotting flesh scarcely buried in shallow graves. Their fate was sealed and rested in the hands of four brutal men. Their bodies would be tossed in a shallow grave to stink and rot, or they might be burned in the crematory pit. The darkness around them was unparalleled with anything they had ever imagined. The abyss of hell was located on this tiny island.

The full sense of greed and power of The Great Ten Nations came full circle to Rachael's mind. She truly was beginning to understand why her compelling desire to save the innocent from the evil clutches of the government had led her to sell almost all she owned and set up a mission of mercy. Evil this strong had to be fought with the power of God, otherwise souls would die and be lost forever in darkness. Her heart was breaking as she walked the dark dirt path. All she worked for, even her faithful allegiance to God, seemed lost.

She kept pace. Michael held tight on her arm.

Looking up into the sky while she walked the path, the heavens were lit with hundreds of twinkling stars, yet on earth the night was black with the curse of sin. All along, her grandfather was right when he told her about the horror that would one day come upon the earth. She never doubted him, but until tonight she had shut it out, charting the stark reality of his words into something far into the future, something that would never come to her. Tears streamed down her face as she remembered his bold exhortations to stay faithful because the end of the Age would be a time never seen or experienced before.

Strange how thoughts race through one's mind when death is impending. She remembered Grant and his enthusiasm to agree with her grandfather's theories. These two men helped to shape her destiny and give her purpose. She felt as though she could almost reach out and touch them. Would she be united with them soon?

She wondered.

As she walked the dark path, accompanied by those whom she had pledged to rescue and keep safe, she suddenly felt a deep sense of affirmation that God had not ordained her mission to end this way. Immediately she forbid herself to consider defeat, as though her spirit needed chastising for doubting.

Who but God would dare to entertain her with such a wild and uncontrollable inspiration, embedding itself into her spirit while the reality of four evil men was bent on killing her? But she kept resisting, thinking that what she needed most was the power to die with dignity, not the hopeless expectation that she would be rescued. Marching a dirt path to the drum of evil power was too great to hope for a miracle. Death was all around her and escaping it was out of the question. She remembered what Rose said the day she picked her up in Troy and took her to the mansion.

"Many will die because of their loyalty to their convictions. Let there be no doubt that this evil thing that has come upon us will not stop until it has destroyed the ethics and morals of even good people."

Looking ahead, and being careful not to fall on the rough pathway, Rachael silently prayed: *Father, I plead with You to save us or take us quickly to be with You.*

When they reached a small clearing, the women and children were told to sit on the ground. The men were forced to stand to one side. The ground was cold and damp. All of them were shivering. Kendall looked at them in pity, wondering if it was shock rather than cold and nerves that was making them shake.

"Move together close," he said to them, hoping that as they nestled close, it would warm them and stave off the dangers of shock.

"It ain't going to matter if they move close or not, American dream boy," the sheriff said to Kendall. "They're gonna get warmed up real soon. So shut up and do what you're told."

He waved his gun at the men and told them to turn and march into the woods. The other three deputies marched with them.

Beyond any reasonable doubt, their intent was to kill the men first and then come after the women and children. Kendall nervously tried to think of a way to overcome the officers, but there was no opportunity to rush at them. He tried to catch the eyes of Martin and Paul. If they rushed the officers, they might be able to overtake them. He wanted to give them a signal, but too concerned about their wives and children, no eye contact was possible.

The women and children sat helpless to do anything except watch as their three beloved men walked at gunpoint into the woods. There were no embraces or goodbyes. Thoughts were racing in everyone's mind, like untamed horses caught in a corral. If ever a time had come in each of their lives to be still and trust God, it needed to arrive now.

As soon as the men and officers were out of sight, Maggie began to recite a passage of scripture from the book of Isaiah in the Old Testament, as near as she could remember it. This was her way of doing things. She was a comforter, the one who took Rachael to her heart when her mother died suddenly. It was her nature to comfort, it was her nature to pray, and it was her nature to quote the words of an Almighty God. She began to speak as though the words were coming straight from the Lord:

"I am He who will comfort you and save you. I am the one who stretched out the heavens, which so often in their glory catch your eyes and cause you to marvel and wonder. I am He who laid the foundation of the earth, and you stand firm upon it without tumbling into outer space. I am the one who churns up the ocean and causes its waves to heave and roar. I allow the great storms and I calm the sea with the sound of my voice. I am the one who has put my Word in your mouth. I have sought and cared for each of you, while you were but babies in your mother's womb, while you were still children, even in the adult years of your life. I won't let go of you now."

It seemed that the door of the Tabernacle of God opened with her words. She knelt on her knees, putting her face to the ground, and began praying. The other women followed her example and scrambled to their knees. It was a scene of pathetic pleading.

Shots rang out, one after another, four of them, then more. It was hard to discern how many because they were coming so close together.

The women stopped praying and listened. Dead silence followed. It was over. Now the evil ones would come for the women and children.

Rachael took Beth into her arms and kissed her. Karen and Laura brought their children close.

Connie and Nathan clung to each other, while Maggie and the other single women huddled close together. No one spoke. Fear and grief were so strong there were no words to be found, yet their hearts beat loud and fast like drums.

"We must be brave," Rachael said in a calm voice. "God will give us the strength to bear whatever is going to happen to us."

"Yes," Maggie whispered. "We are not alone, can't you feel the power that is here?"

"I feel it," Laura said, her voice trembling.

"Yes, it's as though we are enveloped in something strange and wonderful," Karen added. "I'm not afraid anymore."

"What is this?" Rachael questioned, as she observed the children in the dim moonlight and saw that they were no longer crying.

"God has comforted the hearts of these children. Look how brave they are."

Whatever it was that had come and from whence it came, it had the power to quiet fear and give peace. The women and children sat calmly, waiting for the officers to emerge from the woods.

The sound of rustling leaves and snapping twigs broke the silence with footsteps coming closer from the woods. Closer and louder, the sounds came. The moonlight cast faint shadows of approaching officers.

"There's only three of them," Laura whispered. "That's all I can make out. Where's the other officer?"

No one answered; they just sat silently transfixed, watching the shadows of three men coming closer and closer. The snapping and crackling of small twigs beneath their feet inescapably meant that death was fast on its way. It sounded like a hundred stampeding horses. They held their silence and simply sat looking toward the sound, watching in the dim moonlight for the faces of their executioners.

A voice called out from the edge of the woods, but no one could make out what it was saying. Again, it called.

"It's us, don't be afraid!"

No one moved. Not sure what they heard. They sat motionless, waiting for a glimpse of the officers.

Again, the voice called out, this time, though, sounding like more than one.

"Don't be afraid. It's us!"

And then came the glorious sound of a recognizable voice, slicing through the darkness like the sound of a victorious trumpet. It was Kendall's voice, and Rachael recognized it. She let out a curdling screech of joy and scrambled to her feet, looking toward the woods, afraid to move toward the voice for fear it was a trick. Then she saw him running with Paul and Martin.

"It's Kendall," she screamed. "He's alive!"

Out from the shadows of the woods, with a million stars shining above them, as if the glory was enhancing the celebration of God's power, they watched the three figures come forward, their faces illuminated by the rays of the moon. Kendall, Paul, and Martin had miraculously overtaken the officers.

CHAPTER 12
THE BOLD FACE OF CHANGE

THE MURKY SHORELINE AND FOUL stench from shallow graves faded away as they turned the boat around and headed back to Detroit. Everyone was gathered close together at the front of the boat, eager to hear how the police were caught off-guard and their beloved men were able to escape.

"The sheriff stumbled on a large exposed tree root," Paul said in an overly loud voice, so to be heard over the sound of the engine. "I think he may have broken his ankle because he made such a commotion that it brought the other officers rushing to help him."

Martin turned from the captain seat. "It just happened, like something out of the blue," he said. "One moment we were walking, and the next moment the sheriff was on the ground wrenching with pain and his deputies were groping all over him, trying to get him up. Paul grabbed the chance to get a gun off one of the officers. It all happened so fast we hardly had time to think about it."

The boat surged onward, bouncing up and down in the choppy waves of the river channel while they forged their way to the shoreline. The group stayed huddled together to avoid the cold night air. The questions to the men were nonstop. Everyone was talking at once. Kendall continued in a loud voice, "With one gun pointed at the officers, I quickly retrieved the other guns. We had no choice but to shoot them; otherwise, we would all be in eternity at this moment."

The group was silenced with Kendall's words, stunned at the thought of what had taken place in the woods. Death was only moments away at that point.

"I don't know if you caught what I caught from those cops when they were laughing about discovering us. No one knows that they found us," he continued, almost yelling at the top of his voice to be heard over the boat engine. "They were going to report it to the authorities after we were dead and the mansion was pillaged."

After saying that, he got up from his seat and embraced as many of them as he could get into his arms.

"We're free," he bellowed, "we're still free!"

The cheers and joyful crying had to be a sight the angels in heaven were rejoicing over. There could be no doubt in anyone's mind that their rescue was the direct result of God's intervention. Rachael listened without saying much, as she pondered the miracle that moments ago she had almost doubted. She wrapped the blanket around Beth tightly, working to quiet her cries. The baby was hungry, everyone was hungry. They would be home soon. Warm and safe with full bellies.

Lights on Southfield Road finally came into plain view as the boat neared the shoreline. They spotted their vans, still parked where they were left. Martin eased the boat along the dock and turned the engine off, while Kendall jumped off and tied it securely, then carefully helped everyone get onto the dock. Esther was terribly weakened. Paul picked her up and carried her.

They split up into the same two groups they'd formed at the mansion.

"Stay close behind me," Kendall said to Martin, looking at his watch and noting that it was after midnight. "We shouldn't run into much traffic at this hour, but if I see anything suspicious ahead, I'll put my turn signal on, and we'll find another road."

******

The vans slowly turned onto the circle drive in front of the mansion at three o'clock in the morning. Duke came running out from the darkness, barking and wagging his tail. The poor animal had spent the chilly hours locked outside the mansion.

"There he is," Maggie squealed happily. "He knew we would be back."

It took only a few minutes to wake the children and get everyone inside. Kendall and Martin pulled the vans into the garage and out of sight, while Lillian and Connie wasted no time getting hot beverages ready and peanut butter and jelly sandwiches made. Kendall made a quick assessment of Esther and Rose's condition after they finished eating. Both the elderly women appeared to manage the ordeal as well as could be expected for their age and their health. Esther, of course, was weak, but Kendall was more concerned because they were exposed for several hours to the cold night air.

"We're fine, Dr. Saunders," Rose said, as he handed her a couple of aspirins and a glass of water.

"Well, maybe you're fine, but my feet and legs are still cold," Esther told him. "I think I got chilled to the bone."

Kendall took more time with her, hearing some congestion in her lungs through the stethoscope.

"I'm going to put you on antibiotics for a few days just to make sure we don't get into more problems with your lungs," he told her.

Convinced that everyone else had managed the experience without physical problems, he bid them all goodnight. Tomorrow he would check them all again and pay special attention to the children and Esther. Emotional and psychological trauma had greatly affected all of them.

In the weeks to come, its effects might still be with them.

******

The days and weeks passed, leading them into another month. The children emerged from the experience on Mud Island without exhibiting any long-term psychological problems, but Kendall was deeply concerned about Esther, who appeared to be developing full-blown congestive heart failure. He made a point to inform the others of her weakened state.

"She's failing rapidly," he told them confidentially, as if to prepare them that she would soon be winging her way heavenward.

Although their concerns for Esther occupied much of everyone's mind, the business of running the mission continued. Martin and Paul planned to drive to Lansing and barter for food at an open exposition featuring plants and food, located not far from the large campus of Michigan State University. The outdoor event was well advertised on television and would bring hundreds of people into the area. It would be risky to barter, but food was scarce again. There might not be another good opportunity if they did not take advantage of this open exposition. If they could slip inconspicuously into the crowd and barter in the crush of people, they would not be noticed.

The vague promise of finding vegetable seeds also encouraged them to make the trip.

Rachael selected several pieces of jewelry and put them into two small cloth pouches that would be safe in their pockets and easily retrieved during the bartering process. Lillian painstakingly went over what food items were most critical to pick up, dried foods that could be cooked in water would serve as well as canned food, she told them. She reminded them to get flour, oil, and sugar.

"Whatever you see that is even halfway nutritious, get it," she told them. "I'm used to creating miracles in the kitchen with whatever I have to work with."

******

The trip was successful, although it cost them every piece of jewelry in their pockets. They returned with several varieties of dried beans, colorful pasta, rice, jerky, flour, oil, and raw sugar. They even managed to get seeds for carrots and string beans. On the way back, at a small independent grocery store, unexpectedly unattended by the authorities, they bartered for several boxes of powdered milk and twenty cans of evaporated milk. It was an extremely plentiful haul and would carry them well into the planting and growing season.

At dinner that evening, Martin suggested they visit the nearby farmers when they began to plant their cornfields.

"We can ask for any seed they don't use. We don't need much."

"Well, I think that's a great idea," Laura said. "The children can help plant and take care of the garden. It will be a wonderful experience for them and for all of us."

Rachael remembered an old rototiller tucked back in a corner in one of the garages. The maintenance crew used it when the flower gardens were planted years ago. "I'm sure it's still in working condition," she told them.

Things were looking up. They would survive.

******

Kendall woke early. He dressed and grabbed his flashlight to make his usual rounds down the long hallway to check on Rose and Esther. Rose was still asleep, so he pulled her door almost shut and quietly moved on. There was just enough light from Esther's nightlight to see that she was not in bed. He walked into her private bath, and there he found her face-down on the ceramic tiled floor. Although no overhead lights were allowed during dark hours, he frantically flipped on the bathroom light and saw that her lips were blue, and her breathing had stopped. He checked for a carotid pulse. There were no pulsations. Her heart had stopped hours ago. She was cold, and he guessed that she had been dead for some time.

His heart sank in grief, for he had come to love the old lady. She was the feisty personality that gave spark to the group. Her Jewish manners and love for nice things coincided so well with his own background. She could have easily passed for his mother. Swallowing the lump in his throat, he covered her body with a blanket and left to wake Rachael.

ESTHER'S BURIAL WAS HANDLED THE same as her husband's. She was washed and nicely dressed and placed on her bed. Connie fixed her hair and put a light touch of makeup on her face. Paul officiated the funeral rituals, and when night came a grave was dug next to Peter's. Once again, Rachael watched from the kitchen window as the men laid the old woman to rest beside her beloved husband. Her heart was heavy with grief. It was midnight in her soul once again. *Would there be more deaths in the mansion,* she thought to herself? *Would Carson Hill become a cemetery?* It was life she hoped to bring to victims, not a cemetery in her backyard.

******

Paul was successful in coaxing sweet corn seeds from a farmer not far from the mansion. The farmer even offered fertilizer, being amused by Paul's interest in growing vegetables. He had no clue that this Springfield Lake resident was a defector but assumed that he was simply a man with a green thumb and the ambition to grow a garden. Paul was vague about where he lived, making it appear like he owned one of the lakeshore houses.

Martin rigged up some fishing poles from tree limbs. Using needles from Maggie's sewing box and a pair of pliers, he made fish hooks. The public marina at Springfield Lake offered an excellent spot to fish, and trying to catch dinner became a sport that thoroughly thrilled the children. Spring brought many good things. It was unmistakable that Rachael's mission on Carson Hill had made a family out of the twelve that survived. Perhaps midnight had passed and daylight was on the horizon.

Success in Rachael's eyes was not a commencement, for she was wise enough to know that there would be no conclusion for her mission. Every culmination has a new beginning, like planting tulip bulbs and watching them spring forth and bloom. Her continuous pursuit of saving people from tyranny demanded an ongoing chase, with all success being realized for one purpose, the benefit of others for the benefit of God's kingdom that she believed was coming to earth quickly.

Now that her faith was strengthened by the miraculous deliverance from death on Mud Island, Rachael was confident they could hold up well and accommodate every new situation. Her remembrance of something author Leo Buscaglia wrote in his book, *Bus 9 to Paradise*, encouraged her that none of them would regress in the daring face of change. Leo wrote: *Healthy human beings welcome the opportunity to adapt to new experiences. In fact, they're quite comfortable in a constant state of change. They are alive to the possibility of becoming someone new each moment.*[3]

THE WORLD WOULD REMAIN IN the throes of a skirmish that would eventually usher in a dictator. Just how long it would be before the evil oppressor appeared on the world scene was anyone's guess, but he or she would come with hallowed promises and establish a false peace. Exactly what the future held for the residents on Carson Hill could not be known or even guessed at. But for Rachael, her purpose in life had been established by God long before she understood the slippery slope the world was sliding on. Whatever the future held, she was certain it was being held in God's capable hands.

---

3   *Bus 9 to Paradise*, Leo Buscaglia, Slack Publishers, page 107.

CHAPTER 13
APPOINTMENT WITH KISMET

THE SUN WAS BEGINNING TO rise over the distant hills when Rachael walked out on the porch with a cup of coffee and breathed in the thick moist air that carried the wonderful scent of country air. While everyone was still sleeping, her restless spirit quickened with uneasiness. She noticed that it was excessively warm, and there was no breeze to stir the humid morning air, which meant when the sun was overhead, it would turn this August day into a sizzler. However, a scorching summer day was of little concern to the sparrows, chirping as though they were charged with the responsibility of coaxing the sun over the treetops. Sipping the coffee and leaning against one of the massive gothic pillars, she considered all that had taken place in such a short span of time. The US was hardly recognizable now that Chimera was up and controlling everyone's finances. The rest of the world changed as rapidly as the US. The control of The Ten Great Nations was phenomenal because the US was the chief player and author. It was incredible how fast the gigantic computer program ushered in the universal financial system that ruled everyone's pocketbook, even their lives. Turning around and sitting down on one of the white rattan rockers, she continued to sip coffee and relax, if that were possible.

Kendall brought Beth down from their bedroom and placed her in her highchair at the dining room table, tying a bib around her neck and kissing her little cheeks before he sat down. The morning was like most mornings with breakfast served on time and Martin stopping off in the library to turn the television on and get the latest news. But the routine was not going to play out like other mornings, because the news coming across the screen was hair raising.

In big, bold print across the top of the screen were the words NEWS ALERT. At the bottom, the caption read: *Iran launches nuclear bomb and misses Israel and hits Egypt by mistake.* A news anchor was interviewing someone from the Pentagon while bulletins kept flashing across the bottom of the screen.

The Pentagon official looked solemnly into the camera and struggled to stay composed.

"Iran has always been a military concern to the world, but this action comes as a complete surprise to us and the rest of the world."

Martin darted out of the library and into the dining room, white as a ghost and breathing hard. "Iran hit Egypt last night with a nuclear bomb!" he yelled at the top of his voice. Everyone turned and stared at him.

"What?" Kendall questioned as he jumped out of his seat. Martin continued breathlessly talking.

"The news channel is reporting that Iran secretly set out to destroy Israel with a nuclear bomb but missed its target and hit Egypt instead!"

Everyone got up from the table and gathered in the library around the television screen. Rachael was now inside, standing with Maggie listening to the startling news.

"While we wait for the President to speak, we have the Secretary of State with one of our correspondents. Let's listen to what he has to say," the news anchor said.

"Mr. Secretary," the correspondent began, "can you tell us just how crucial this incident is to the rest of the world and if you see repercussions coming from other nations?"

Holding the microphone close to the Secretary's mouth, the conversation continued: "It's very serious. We expect nations surrounding Egypt will get revved up for military action, especially Israel. We anticipate China and Russia to do nothing, and they may defend Iran's action. Everything depends on the extent of retaliation around the world. At this point, the US is standing silent until all information is gathered."

Rachael moved closer to the television and turned to address the residents, all astonished and showing fear.

"This is likely to turn into World War III," she said in a calm voice that hid the concern and fear she was experiencing. "We have talked about the end coming for the nations, and how a Divine plan for mankind will eventually bring everything and everyone into peaceful subjection. We need not be afraid. We know whatever comes, the life we will have beyond the life we have now will be wonderful. All we need at this point is to pray and keep listening to the news reports. I'm not going to soft-soap this, not even for the children. We are likely facing the end of the world as we know it. We must stay strong and help each other."

In many ways, her speech sounded like words coming from a leader of a religious cult, instructing its people to prepare for death. Yet, there was no hysterical preaching or distorted doctrine being taught. What was evident in this group of survivors of Chimera was unity in the belief that evil had taken over the world, and God would deal with it. They were not a bunch of religious kooks awaiting a cosmic asteroid to make an appearance in outer space and snatch them up and carry them off to some utopia where they would live as interplanetary beings. On the contrary, they believed what was penned by the Prophets of old, who were inspired to write what was given to them by God. Those prophecies clearly spelled out that the end would come someday, and it would come by forced hostility from nations exercising furious evil toward one another.

Paul made his way to the center of the group standing in front of the television.

"The course that the United States has been traveling for the past forty years is no different from that of Sodom and Gomorrah. It seems to me that judgment day has arrived. I wish I could say for certain that our nation will not be annihilated along with other nations if war becomes full blown, but I can't. Our nation has sold their souls to the devil. Consequences are deserved."

Sensing that the children had heard enough, Kendall interrupted, "Well, let's go back into the dining room and have our breakfast. The news media will report what the President has to say in a few minutes, and we can talk about this after we are nourished."

******

The news throughout the day was troubling. The President did not take stern opposition toward Iran in his televised remarks; instead he chastised Israel for provoking their neighbors. The United Nations called an emergency meeting to discuss the situation, but they simply mimicked the President's attitude. No nation or political figure was in a hurry to console Egypt and discipline Iran. It was shaping up that a secret plot had been made to have the US stand down. The conclusion for Rachael and the Carson Hill residents was that the President was joining Iran, Russia, and the Arab countries in an effort to stop Israel from building houses and increasing their territory within the Palestinian settlements, moreover, to wipe them off the map. What seemed obvious was that Jerusalem would be given to the Palestinians. As soon as the Middle East and Russia allied with each other, Europe and Great Britain would retaliate, not because of their love for Israel, but to stop the power machine of which the US President was the leader.

The Ten Great Nations were fast coming to nothing, zilch, as this new alliance emerged with this sudden nuke lobbed into Egypt.

The children were scurried into the library to play while the adults gathered in the grand room to discuss the world situation.

"I agree with Rachael that we are heading for World War III," Paul said, settling into a comfortable chair.

"I do too," Martin said frankly. "Once the nukes start flying, there will be massive destruction and pollution. We won't escape. No one will. Even China has nuclear missiles that can reach our country. It's obvious that our President is siding with Russia, and although China has not been mentioned, they are in cahoots with them. Let's face it, the President whitewashed this aggressive action, rather than speak words that would comfort us and lead us to believe he is protecting our country. I would wager a bet that he will leave as soon as he gets word that the bombs and missiles are ready to launch. He's got a hiding place somewhere, and he will take his evil administration with him. The Americans that survive will become their pawns, that is, if there are survivors."

Everything was playing out as foretold thousands of years ago. The world has laughed and said it would never happen, but now the great Euphrates River was as dry as a bone, and China was preparing to send two million troops toward Israel. They would travel the river path. Russia and Iran, along with other Arab nations, were almost ready to launch their nuclear weapons upon North America and then take possession of Israel. The revival of a new and terrifying Empire was about to emerge.

The group sat for hours into the night, talking and fitting the biblical puzzle together. They agreed that some in the world would say it was God who created this horrible mess, the mess being brought to a climax and everything destroyed must come from none other than a harsh Creator that hates instead of loves. But in the final analysis, history shows that it is mankind that devours itself, not God. If the gathering at Megiddo is not the basic result of man's evil heart, then it would have to be symbolic of a war against Christ.

******

The summit at Megiddo continued for days. The press was there but kept everything that transpired a secret. The US kept standing mute. Europe was playing it cool and staying alert, but also quiet. No one wanted to risk all-out nuclear war. Very little was being reported. Egypt had been literally wiped off the map. The devastation and death were insurmountable. Those who survived the blast fled deep into Africa. The world appeared to be standing down in a mysterious hold. Hell was waiting.

Prayers in the grand room grew more intense. God was the only hope for survival. No one was telling wonderful stories. No one laughed or joked. No one was singing. A deep, gnawing sense of uncertainty was invading the peace they once knew.

In quiet moments when Rachael could think and contemplate, she wondered why, if the world was destined to come to this, had she gone to all the trouble and effort to turn her life upside down by creating a rescue mission for victims of Chimera? Why had she sold the Carson Real Estate Corporation and let go of all the things she loved if it would come to this? Why was closing herself up in this country mansion and waiting for death worth only a year of survival? Nothing made sense if she looked at the situation from human reasoning. Yet deep inside her soul, the plan to save victims from a world gone mad had to be preordained. There must be a reason, or else she was crazy.

******

Ten days passed, and it was now early September. The world was still quiet in a mysterious hold. It was another uncertain evening. The children were in bed, including Beth in her crib upstairs. Lillian brewed fresh lemon and ginger tea and brought it to the grand room, where another night of prayer and conversation would last until everyone was emotionally worn and ready to retire for the night.

"I would love one of those sugar cookies you made yesterday if there are any left," Martin said.

"Yes, there are, I'll get some of them," Lillian responded.

"Is that thunder?" Laura asked, looking at Martin sitting next to her on the couch.

"I don't think so. We're not supposed to have rain until tomorrow."

Again, a thundering sound came from the distance, and with this clap, the windows of the mansion rattled. Immediately Kendall got up and walked into the entrance hall and opened the front double doors. There was a glow in the eastern sky like that of fire from burning trash or wood. Martin walked into the entrance hall.

"What is it?" he questioned.

"I don't know. Maybe a gas or chemical explosion."

Before he could say anything else, Martin interrupted. "Well, either that or we are being hit by the enemy!"

The entire group was now standing in the entrance hall, looking out from the large open mahogany doors. They waited for more sounds.

"Well, whatever it was, it seems to have stopped," Kendall remarked, ushering everyone back inside.

Martin, always with an ear for news, headed for the library and turned on the television. The news channel was reporting that North Korea launched two warhead missiles aimed at the US; the first hitting New York and the second over-reaching its target and landing in Jackson, Michigan."

"Well, now we know what we were seeing," he said, his voice quivering because the threat of full-blown war was evident. The news anchor went on, while the rest of the group came into the library.

"The Associated Press is reporting that the President and his Administration boarded Air Force I early this morning and are at an undisclosed location. Pentagon officials are directing governors to take full charge of their states and move to their emergency plans.

"Can you believe that?" Martin said almost with a tone of anger, turning around and looking at the rest of the group. "The President knew this was coming. He has sold us to the devil!"

The television screen was filled with pictures panning New York City. It was a scene hundreds of times worse than 9/11. The news anchor spoke again.

"Government Aids are reporting that no one is in command in Washington. Congress is unreachable. Officials at the Pentagon are directing state governors to employ their emergency plans immediately."

"So what do we do now?" Lillian asked, looking at Rachael. "Sure can't run to the cubby in the basement. It's been demolished."

"I would suggest that the women go to their bedrooms and lie close to their children," she said soberly. "I'm not sure the basement is any safer than anywhere else in the mansion. I think the men should stay here on the first floor and listen to news reports. Not that it will help our situation, but they can stay informed as things progress. The children have not awakened. Let's just stay close to them. Rose, come into my bedroom and stay with Beth and me.

Before starting up the stairway, Rachael turned and said, "The members of Congress are no doubt dead, or being held somewhere against their will."

No one commented. Everyone was too shocked to say anything. Paul picked up a Bible and sat down in the office chair, while Kendal and Martin sat on the leather couch. He started reading about a city that was dressed in fine linen, purple and scarlet with gold and jewels. "This city," he said, "is going to be destroyed, and I believe it's us."

******

Laura rested next to her twin sons. She listened to their soft breathing, wondering if the night would pass safely. Karen lay sleepless, close to her children. She muffled her crying so she would not wake them. Fear clamped down hard on her, so heavy she felt she could not breathe. Connie was cuddled close to Nathan. All the children were safe with their mothers.

Rachael felt numb, as though she had no emotion left to experience. She picked up Beth from the crib, wrapped her in a blanket, and laid her gently on the bed. She turned off the nightlight, then felt her way to the bed. Still wearing the clothes she had worn all day. Lying motionless next to Rose and baby Beth, she stared into the darkness.

Maggie and Lillian were in their quarters on the third floor, huddled in one bedroom. It was as safe up there as it would be anywhere in the mansion.

Downstairs the television went black, and all the low lights throughout the mansion went off. Across one-fourth of the globe, the same thing was happening. Everything was going black. Electromagnetic bombs were blasted high in the world's atmosphere, creating powerful microwaves that fried computers, blinded radar, and silenced radios and televisions. As soon as the E-bombs completed their penetrations, four nuclear bombs were released. The hits were made on the US, Great Britain, Israel, and Germany. Iran and Russia and China leaned back in their control seats.

Simultaneously, surprise nuclear bombs from the north side of Israel came whooshing into the territories of Iran, Russia, and China. Astronauts in the space station saw the earth burning like a fireball. The appointment with kismet had come. The world resembled what the sight of hell must be. Only in the imagination of the mind could one speculate if there would be any survivors.

******

It was morning. The same rhythmic tempo of sunlight that woke Rachael from sleep the morning she slid her hands across the silk sheets to touch Grant, but found him missing, was again cascading across the rolling knolls of the Irish Hills. Like aerobic waves rising and falling, it swept again over Carson Hill. Was it a miracle or a chance happening that Rachael and her people stood on the front porch of the mansion, awake and unhurt, looking out upon Springfield Lake in wonderment that they were alive and the mansion stood strong?

CHAPTER 14

IN THE TWINKLING OF AN EYE

MORNING CAME AS THOUGH THE sun was forced to keep shining.

"Let's not kid ourselves, it's not going to get better," Martin said to the Carson Hill residents who were coddling their fears as if all their coping mechanisms were lost at sea.

"We can't just sit here traumatized. We have to come up with a plan to survive."

The nuclear attack hung a massive cloud of fear and confusion over the world. Every person who was wounded, dying, or safe was in shock. No one had a clue if there was a victor or a global figure taking charge. It would be months before bombed countries would recover. The most imminent question that was concerning the residents on Carson Hill was how damaging the nuclear fallout was to them? Would they become sick and die? In the hours and days that followed the attack, the group sat in the mansion praying and debating the questions.

"I believe this is the last warning and the last invitation for people to get their lives straightened out and their hearts right with God," Rose said. "I believe He allowed these attacks for that reason."

It would be hard for people who were suffering and who lost loved ones to see this catastrophe as a justifiable warning from God and an invitation to repent, but in view of Carson Hill's miraculous survival, God was obviously in control, and perhaps grace was still available to the lost. The same inherent thirst that brought each of them to Christ was hopefully still at work in the heart of mankind. The deep hunger for something beyond their meaningless narcissistic existence surely was keeping them searching for God at this moment. He was the One they longed for, though it would take time for them to know this.

As for Maggie, she would never forget the conviction she felt about her personal sins and how she longed for something beyond herself, something outside the empty future that awaited her in ghettos when she was but a teenager. Perhaps decades ago it was easier to find the Lord, but that question had no relevance to a God who was always the same, yesterday, today, and forever. He was no harder or easier to find today than He was decades ago. But in view of the fact that the world was now being operated under the dictatorship of an evil group of leaders, who caused the sudden war in the Mediterranean, man's conviction about sin seemed absent. Society had long ago been lulled to sleep by the lies of the evil elite. So, they were witnessing the inevitable.

In prior years the United Nations and the US Supreme Court created enormous confusion over the right and wrong of human character. Vital questions regarding moral conduct were treated with complacency. Political correctness was the new code of ethics. Then the game became the need to win, rather than operate by the truth. Progressive ideology was successfully overhauling conservatism.

THE GROUP ASSEMBLED IN THE grand room after a lean dinner of canned spaghetti and corn muffins. Rachael had plenty to say because she knew what they faced was hardcore end-time reality.

"What we Christians have been fighting the last twenty-five years is the ideology of revolutionists, whose philosophies are Marxist," she commented. "Their way of thinking was to divide, oppress, and conquer. It is really communism when it is analyzed correctly."

She went on, "My parents sensed there were ideologies within Congress back in the late fifties that were leaning toward socialism, probably even before then. Immorality and materialism were driving everything, a steak on every grill and two cars in every garage and raunchy movies every weekend."

She could dare to talk like this because her parents had worked hard and honest for their wealth, and they were honorable Christian people. She kept talking while Lillian passed coffee to everyone.

"I didn't understand it at first because I was only in grade school, but I did see during my teenage years a godlessness developing in our nation. By the time I was a well-seasoned adult, I was witnessing a nation falling into the throes of liberalism that not only had invaded both Political Parties of our Congress, but the Church as well. The progressive ideology was actually served up from the White House in the last few years, and we have witnessed a burgeoning push to destroy our Constitution.

"I'm telling it like it is, dear friends. I sensed this destruction even before this new Chimera tyranny came into existence. Leaders have been lying to us and concealing their true agendas. What they wanted was to recreate the American individual. The plan was to give the progressive left, and The Ten Great Nations, the right to create new rules and change the social order in America and the entire world. I see it as the work of Satan."

She went on speaking, taking a sip of coffee every now and then.

"Let's take a hard look at it right now, while we are trying to figure out what our next strategy for surviving will be. All of us in this room believe that revolutionary change in our country, and in the world, came about first by giving the masses hope along with the lie that all they desired could truly become theirs. The leaders promised change, deliverance, a new movement.

"What amazes me the most is that Americans could not see what was going on. To be perfectly honest, without sounding pious, very few can discern evil for what it really is. The final goal of the progressive left was to eliminate class identification and create world communism. These people hate God, so therefore they hate what is good. They hate us. How well we know that when we were forced to ride in our vans to Mud Island. We are sheep amidst the wolves."

She paused to allow questions.

Martin spoke up, asking the ultimate question: "Well, it looks to me that we are pretty well doomed. So, who can rescue America now that Satan has the foothold? Better yet, who can save the world?"

Paul, being the one most educated in the Scriptures, eagerly broke into the conversation to answer that question.

"I don't think any of us can save America or the world. I believe only the Rapture of the Believers will save Christians from this tyranny. After that, it will be the return of Jesus Christ who saves this world."

To those in the grand room who were steeped in the knowledge of the Bible, the event of the Rapture was their hope, that great snatching away of the Christians, especially now under conditions of this present catastrophic happening. To believe, at any moment, they might be suddenly caught up in the air to be with Christ forever was what gave the antiestablishment Christians the hope they needed to keep going.

A groan came from Connie as the reality of what had been discussed sank in. Surviving the last several months had been the worst difficulty of her life, yet she wished they still had those options open, to live undercover, to barter for food, and survive, if only for the sake of the children.

Sensing everyone's despair, Paul spoke up, "The past cannot be retrieved. The good and the bad in it will never be ours again, and that's a good thing because the present and the future is what belongs to us. Each day we live is new. What happens depends on our free will choices and God's control."

******

As it happened, cable television in the Eastern Time zone suddenly went black when network electronics fried like burnt toast. A few local stations were still televising, but the best source of news came from radio. Newscasters reported that New York City and Cleveland, Ohio were literally wiped out. The nuke lobbed into Cleveland was aimed at Washington, D.C., but missed the target, veering northwest and landing just shy of Lake Erie in downtown Cleveland. The enemy's aim was perfect in New York, coming down smack in the middle of Manhattan Island.

Years ago, there was both mercy and a future warning on September eleventh when the US Trade Centers were attacked. Churches from east to west and north to south were filled the following Sunday with people turning their attention to God and suddenly getting religion. The US experienced a huge Jesus moment. Days later, however, only those who worked to clear the rubble and bury the dead were still praying. The nation went back to its narcissistic behavior, filling their stomachs, dulling their minds with strong drink and drugs, and filling their eyes with evil imaged movies. Once again, the nation was avoiding God.

But there was something different about this present catastrophic event, at least for Christians, it appeared different. Copious amounts of end-time prophecy were fulfilled when the implementation of Chimera worldwide occurred. Without a qualm, it seemed that Armageddon was right around the corner. Theologians had been taking to the airways every day, warning the world that the end was here. For the residents on Carson Hill, the end was close, but not always due to the animus threat of Armageddon, but because the food shelves thinned again and again.

******

The days and nights kept wearing on. Sleep was hard to get hold of. Long hours were spent together in the grand room. Faith was generating calm, but slumber was not yielding to their keyed-up minds and anxious spirits. On this particular evening, Lillian brought small dishes of Jell-O into the grand room, thinking a tasty chilled treat would perk up spirits as well as the palette.

"Make no mistake about it," Kendall said, swallowing a spoonful of Jell-O, "we have heard from God. We have survived this nuclear attack, but there is more coming. Still, I am positive we will not be here when this country is completely destroyed. We will be with our Lord."

For a moment, the sound of spoons clicking in the small glass dishes seemed bizarre after a statement of such overwhelming conviction. Shouldn't they be on their knees, praying?

Paul set his empty dish down on the marble stand next to the arm of the chair. He swallowed, moistened his lips, and took up the conversation.

"This is only the beginning. When God gets enough of the sins being committed in this country, it will be complete destruction. We have lived deliciously since the end of World War II. We have sat like a queen for all the world to see. But in a moment, much like what has just happened, death on a level never seen before shall come upon this country."

The talk was severe, but the insight was spot on. What remained evident to everyone on Carson Hill was that chunks of biblical prophecy had been fulfilled right before their eyes, and the reality of it made their ability to know and understand the present and the future more clearly.

Laura, who generally sat mute during the evening discussions, spoke up with an obvious vengeance in her voice, as though weighing everything in the balances and coming forth with a definite conclusion.

"We have been forced to barter for food because the evil ones have taken it from us, but they will mourn for food and crawl on their stomachs because their hunger will be worse in every respect."

Around the room was a consensus, even an obvious demeanor of recompense for evil. Laura was not alone in her feelings. Honest reasoning for recompense seemed justifiable, considering all they had gone through in the past months. Although God is the avenger, justice wanted its way in the hands of the persecuted.

She continued to speak, as though she had entered into cognizant awareness for the first time since coming to the mission.

"The most valuable thing in everyone's life is truth. If the truth is fully known and realized, the world would change. It is the false illusions that people practice that take them down. By that I mean, those who live in their own universe of desire become self-indulgent and vulnerable. They are void of the truth. It takes very little persuasion to push them over into believing a bogus lie, which is what we saw happening when Chimera was implemented worldwide. The world believed the fairy tale the leaders of The Ten Great Nations were peddling. The masses were easily indoctrinated into their idiotic plan for a financial system worldwide.

She went on talking, as though something powerfully strong was impaling her.

"We didn't go for the lies because we knew the truth. So in many respects, the truth set us free, but in another respect, our individual freedom to practice our Christian beliefs put us in jeopardy of persecution. We quickly discovered that the era in which the world exists is anti-God and anti-Christian. It is basically pro-self, and that is the reason the entire world was duped into the scheme of Chimera. The promise the world swallowed was a fairy tale.

"The world is getting their just deserts. Man eventually will take down man.

"I am angry, yes, because of the persecution and suffering that Christians are enduring. At the same time, I am also avenged knowing that what awaits these dreaming anti-God zealots is their full reward."

"THEIR FULL REWARD" WERE THE last three words uttered. The conversation stopped at that point. The room went silent. A mysterious hush silenced the entire atmosphere, like a speechless tryst becoming the triumphant mark of the moment. Silence. Mysterious, peculiar silence throughout the mansion. In other places of the world, the same was happening. In the twinkling of an eye, every Christian was gone. RAPTURED. Taken up to be with the Lord. The prophesied and predicted event that people laughed about and said would never happen, happened.

In the middle of the grand room, a Bible lay on the floor, opened to the pages of the next events. Anyone pilfering the mansion would stumble upon it. The prophecy written thousands of years before, still alive, still warning. The pleas for repentance, the promise of eternal life, every word still there, still breathing.

"ALAS, ALAS, FOR THAT GREAT city! She made us all rich from her great wealth. And now in a single hour all is gone. But you, O heaven, rejoice over her fate, and you, O children of God and the prophets and the apostles! For at last God has given judgment against her for you. Then a mighty angel picked up a boulder shaped like a millstone and threw it into the ocean and shouted, "Babylon, that great city, shall be thrown away as I have thrown away this stone, and she shall disappear forever. Never again will the sound of music be there – no more pianos, saxophones, and trumpets. No industry of any kind will ever again exist there, and there will be no more milling of the grain. Dark, dark will be her nights; not even a lamp in a window will ever be seen again. No more joyous wedding bells and happy voices of the bridegrooms and the brides. Her businessmen were known around the world and she deceived all nations with her sorceries. And she was responsible for the blood of all the martyred prophets and the saints . . . After this I heard the shouting of a vast crowd in heaven, "Hallelujah! Praise the Lord! Salvation is from our God. Honor and authority belong to him alone, for his judgments are just and true. He has punished the Great Prostitute who corrupted the earth with her sin and he has avenged the murder of his servants."[4]

---

4   Revelation 18:19 through 19:3, *The Living Bible* paraphrased, Tyndale Publishers, Wheaton, Illinois, 1971, page 1017.

FROM THE AUTHOR

GOD LOVES YOU AND HAS a plan for your life. The Bible says, "God loved the world so much that He gave His one and only Son, Jesus Christ, that whoever believes in Him shall not perish, but have eternal life" (John 3:16).

We have all sinned and need forgiveness. Jesus died for our sins. He took our place on the cross that we could have a right standing with God. If you have never put your faith in Jesus Christ, and want to be saved by God's grace in Jesus His Son, I invite you to pray this prayer and accept Jesus as your Savior.

Pray this prayer now.

"Dear God, I realize that I am a sinner. I ask for Your forgiveness. I believe that Jesus is truly Your Son who died in my place that I can be saved. I want to put my full trust in Him as my Lord and Savior. I want to follow Him. Take charge of my life now, and help me to do Your will. I pray this in the name of Jesus Christ." Amen.

IF YOU HAVE PRAYED THIS prayer, God wants you to grow in His grace. Begin by reading the Bible. I suggest starting in the Gospel of John, in the New Testament.

God bless you as you daily seek to do God's will and seek His plan for your life.

For more information about
Mary Cates
and
Hidden in Irish Hills
please visit:

www.marycatesauthor.com

For more information about
AMBASSADOR INTERNATIONAL
please visit:

www.ambassador-international.com
@AmbassadorIntl
www.facebook.com/AmbassadorIntl

Thank you for reading this book. Please consider leaving us a review on your favorite retailer's website, Goodreads or Bookbub, or our website.

www.ingramcontent.com/pod-product-compliance
Lightning Source LLC
Chambersburg PA
CBHW072350020726
47506CB00004B/1091